Works in Progress

BRYAN J. DICKERSON

ISBN-13: 978-1797003337

Printed by Kindle Direct Publishing, an Amazon.com Company

OTHER BOOKS BY BRYAN J. DICKERSON

The Liberators of Pilsen: The U.S. Army 16th Armored Division in World War Two Czechoslovakia

*Marine General from the Ranks:
The Life of Lt Gen Homer L. Litzenberg Jr.*

Modern Saints and Blesseds of the Catholic Church

The Organized Marine Corps Reserve in World War Two

An Anthology of Military and Cold War History

History of Marine Wing Support Squadron 472

CONTENTS

INTRODUCTION

Over the years, I have researched and written numerous articles and several books on non-fiction topics, primarily history and religion. I have also dabbled in fiction. This book is a compilation of my fiction writings. None of these stories have been published previously. Several stories were submitted for publication and rejected, and the remainder were not submitted at all. Several of these stories may form the basis of some future novel that I may write. There is no overarching theme or organizational scheme. It is just a collection of fictional pieces that I have written over the last twenty years.

1 IN RUINS

With a fury that had not been experienced in several decades, the hurricane battered the Jersey Shore, inundating large areas of the coastal environs with storm surge and tidal flooding. Wind and water collaborated to forever alter dozens of communities up and down the coast.

Yet amidst this tumultuous unprecedented destruction, one man sat placidly and nearly oblivious to the momentous events occurring all around him. The man's name was David Smith. He was twenty-five-years-old, two inches under six feet tall and sporting an un-athletic build. He now sat in a reclining chair a few feet from a large sliding glass door on the second floor of an expensive oceanfront home in the barrier island community of Sea Isle City, Cape May County, New Jersey. Somehow, David had managed to evade the mandatory evacuation orders and the vigorous police efforts which sought to keep people out of the storm's clutches. Like countless other structures, the home in which he lounged was suffering the ill effects of the unexpected meteorological monster. In his hand, David held a bottle of Yuengling Lager.

The bottle of Yuengling, however, was not the reason for his obliviousness to the storm raging around him. The bottle was a mere means of passing the time. David's mind was far, far away from his present reality and was completely unaffected by the hops, barley and water which infrequently passed through his lips.

Three days before, David Smith had abruptly moved out of his apartment in Philadelphia and stowed his possessions in a self-storage facility. The day before that, David Smith had unexpectedly quit his job as a manager with a health insurance provider in Center City. The evening before that, David had heard the cataclysmic words from his fiancée's lips that he never expected to hear: "I don't love you. I never did love you."

As he sat staring out into the raging storm, David reflected upon all that had transpired in his life and caused him to be here at this particular moment in time in the midst of the worst storm to strike the Jersey Shore in decades.

On an afternoon nearly three years ago, a chance encounter on a subway platform at the 15th/16th and Locust Street Station had sent David Smith's life careening in a direction that he had never envisioned. One irresistible, unexpected force had dramatically altered the trajectory of his future, both personally and professionally.

Her name was Nicole Sussman. She was a senior at the University of Pennsylvania. She was five feet, eight inches tall, with long brown hair and startlingly green eyes. She had a physical radiance that captivated most men around her and a charm that beguiled the rest. She was born of wealth and privilege --- the daughter of the famed neurosurgeon Dr. Nathan Sussman and a de facto only child as a result of a painful divorce. Her mother had moved on and Nicole felt no kinship to a younger brother and sister that her mother had had with another man. Perhaps in an effort to mitigate her disrupted childhood, Nicole's father lavished her in a lifestyle that made her expectant of the finer things in life. Nicole was a Marketing major but that degree would only serve to mark time until she entered into a marriage that could sustain her appetite for luxury and adoration. She came from a privileged class that was descended from privileged class; indeed she could claim descent from a minor baron in the Burgundy region of 17th Century France.

David Smith, in stark contrast, was seemingly one whom Nicole would never give a second look at under normal circumstances. He was of above average height, above average intelligence but below average personal appearance. He was not ugly but certainly not on par with the physical attributes of Nicole Sussman. He was also a college senior studying archaeology at Temple University, and barely affording tuition there. Unlike Nicole, David's devoted parents could not afford to pay his tuition as well as those of his siblings and so he worked part-time to help out with the costs. In his lineage, he could claim descent from a poor farmer who left County Kilkenny, Ireland during the devastating Potato Famine in 1845.

When compared, the contrasts between Nicole and David seemed insurmountable. Yet, for reasons unknown even to himself, David found himself doing the unthinkable for a man of his status and his position.

David initiated a conversation with Nicole as they waited on the subway platform.

Somehow, David managed to muster charm enough to interest the usually uninterested femme fatale and hold Nicole's notoriously fleeting attention while they waited for their respective subway trains. When hers arrived before his, he abruptly changed his afternoon's plans and accompanied her aboard her subway. Thus was the first of many 'change in plans' that David would make in the pursuit of happiness with Nicole.

David had spent much of his life pursuing a career in archaeology. It began with a thirst for adventure inspired by the famed Indiana Jones movies but matured into a more mature, scholarly pursuit of past civilizations through their physical remains and artifacts. Had he had the financial resources, he would have attended the University of Pennsylvania for its world-renown archaeology and anthropology program. Instead, he attended Temple University and satisfied his thirsts for antiquities with frequent visits to the astounding collections at the Penn Museum. He had a particular fondness for pre-Columbian Mesoamerica. In the summer preceding his senior year, he had been fortunate to participate in an archaeological excavation of Mayan ruins in Belize.

But the prospect of further scholarly riches in the jungles of

Central America succumbed to the prospect of future romantic riches with Nicole Sussman. Just as the entangling tropical vegetation of Mesoamerica had swallowed up the magnificent Mayan edifices, so too did the romantic entanglements of Nicole Sussman swallow up David Smith's dreams of re-discovering lost Mayan ruins.

In no time, David and Nicole were in love. None of their friends and family could explain the chemistry between them, nor could they explain it themselves, but apparently it was real nonetheless. Both Nicole and David graduated two months later from their respective colleges. Despite his laissez faire approach to Nicole's social and spending habits, her father forbid the couple to co-habitat before marriage. As her only source of income, it was a demand that Nicole could not ignore. Nevertheless, they were soon living together in all but name.

Had Nicole's father been a lawyer or businessman or politician of some sort, David would likely have found employment with her father's firm or through his connections. But Dr. Sussman, being a neurosurgeon, possessed an immense knowledge base and skill set and worked in a profession that was completely incompatible with David's academic credentials and previous work experience. Nor was Dr. Sussman inclined to offer any career assistance to his daughter's near impoverished boyfriend. So David, in desperate need of the financial resources to fund his love affair with the financially voracious Nicole, sought and obtained employment in the health insurance industry.

Though lacking any academic or professional exposure to the business world, David proved remarkably adaptable to his new chosen career field. Motivation, perseverance and ambition were never in short supply with David and so he applied these traits to mastering the health insurance business. Propelled by the need to acquire wealth, David drove himself to succeed and was periodically rewarded by his appreciative employer. He routinely volunteered to work overtime and studied the insurance business in his free moments to better know his new career. His efforts soon caught the attention of his superiors. His first salary raise came after six months on the job and his first title promotion with a raise after ten months.

Nicole also had found employment, due to a friend of her father's. But her corporate experience was far more relaxed than David's. Her efforts got her a paycheck and little more and she was content with that, as her father still was financing her lifestyle. Her social life remained largely undiminished by her career. She still spent money lavishly and enjoyed life to the fullest. Her appearances at the South Street night spots were only slightly less frequent than when she was at UPenn. She spent summer weekends at her father's Shore house in Sea Isle City, went skiing in Vermont during the winter, and periodically vacationed at Miami Beach when the mood struck her.

David shared in Nicole's adventures as much as he was able to. His self-imposed long work hours significantly diminished his available time with Nicole. When he was with her, David spent prodigious sums of his hard-earned cash in a quixotic quest to satiate her insatiable materialism.

By the end of his second year, David had doubled his starting salary --- not counting performance bonuses, and was serving as an entry level manager with responsibility for a team of seven junior underwriters. Recognizing his obvious talent and determination, his superiors encouraged his ambition and provided him with opportunities for further advancement. It was an impressive accomplishment for someone who had been trained to sift through shards of pottery and stone in search of an elusive past.

Unfortunately, David's meteoric rise up the corporate ladder was not nearly meteoric enough for his intended fiancée. His career advancement and his driving ambition increasingly reduced the time he had available for Nicole, and worse yet in her mind, was not producing the financial dividends fast enough. She knew that someday she would not be able to rely completely on her father's money and she doubted that David could ever earn enough on his own to adequately support her in the life that she was accustomed to.

And so with the careful, disconnected calculation of a surgeon removing a tumor, Nicole uttered the infamous words that struck David's world with catastrophic force and triggered a chain of events which deposited him on the second floor of a summer home in the path of a ferocious hurricane. He could never earn the money required to maintain Nicole in her lifestyle. Much like Francisco Coronado, there was no 'Cibola,' no 'Seven Cities of Gold' with which David could finance a marriage and prolonged life with Nicole.

*   *   *

A couple days later, the property owners of Sea Isle City were allowed to return to the battered community to ascertain the extent of the hurricane's damage upon their homes, businesses and properties.   Among those making their way through the debris strewn streets of Sea Isle City were Dr. Nathan Sussman and his daughter Nicole.

At last they came to their summer home.   Initially they were relieved. The structure of the home appeared to be largely intact. Only a few shingles had blown off the roof and none of the plywood boards protecting the windows had been compromised. But their relief turned to despair as they noticed that the front door of their home had been blown open and some of its contents had been washed out into the front yard.

Warily, Doctor Sussman and his daughter entered their battered home. Apparently the storm surge had penetrated the ocean side of the house and wreaked havoc inside. Furniture, appliances and anything else that could not be moved to the upper floor had been tossed about. A thick layer of wet sand and marine detritus coated the expensive floors and carpets.

Leaving her father to inspect the damage on the ground floor, Nicole ascended a set of stairs and entered into the second story living room. In remarkable contrast to the lower floor, this room was virtually undisturbed. She looked towards the far end of the room where bright sunlight shone in through the sliding glass door that opened onto the outside deck. She noted that the plywood board covering the sliding glass door to the outside deck was missing and surmised that the wind had blown it off.

Then Nicole realized something else was amiss. A reclining chair had been moved near to the sliding glass door. Next to it was an empty six-pack of beer, two empty water bottles and a half-eaten box of donuts. With much alarm, she discovered that there was a figure slumped in the chair. "David?!... *David*, what are you doing here?" she cried out in bewilderment.

The sound of her voice shook David from his stupor. He looked towards her, his eyes struggling to focus for a few seconds. Then he stood.

"David, what are you doing here?" she repeated, adding, "How long have you been here?"

"Oh... I was just leaving," he replied nonchalantly. He breezed past her, adding, "I've got a plane to the Yucatan to catch."

Hearing his daughter's yell, Dr. Sussman hurried up the stairs. David met him about halfway down the stairs. "Good morning Dr. Sussman. You're looking well today," he casually remarked without stopping to offer anything further.

Nicole overcame her shock at seeing David sitting unexpectedly in the living room of her hurricane-damaged summer home and ran after him. She rushed down the stairs, through a hallway and out onto the front porch.

"David, come back here! David, what are you doing? DAVID!!!" she yelled out after him.

But David continued calmly walking on down the debris filled street and out into his future, never once looking back on the love that was no more.   His future happiness once again lay in the Mayans' buried past.

2 ON A SUPERINTENDENT'S SALARY

Brad Rotelli woke up at 7:15 am in the second floor master bedroom of his Westville Beach, Connecticut home. His wife barely stirred as he got out of bed. As usual, Diana Adams-Rotelli would not get out of bed for another two hours, then she'd spend her day socializing with friends or working on her paintings in her private studio on the first floor. The couple had no children nor any desire to have any either.

Brad Rotelli was forty-seven, six-feet tall, 175 pounds with balding hair and a mid-section that had seen better days. His complexion was tanned, the result of a week spent lounging at his vacation home in the Florida Keys earlier that month. He stretched, then quietly made his way across the lavish bedroom to the master bedroom's spacious bathroom and performed his morning hygiene rituals.

Emerging twenty minutes later from the bathroom, Brad Rotelli next went over to his walk-in closet. He opened the door and entered into a cavernous closet filled with expensive Italian suits, shirts, shoes and accoutrements. Pondering his options for a few moments, Rotelli decided upon a $2,100 five-buttoned dark gray pinstripe suit by Italian designer Antonio Manelli. He then selected a pink silk shirt, magenta silk tie, and $400 black leather Fiesso loafer shoes. So as not to wake up his still sleeping wife, Rotelli dressed in the closet.

Within a few minutes, Brad Rotelli exited the closet and left his bedroom. He walked down a long hallway adorned with a variety of his wife's paintings, chuckling to himself as he glanced at the amateurish work that his wife had slaved over for weeks at a time. She had quit her job working as a dental hygienist several years ago to focus full-time on her art. Outwardly he was supportive of his wife's endeavors, but privately he mocked her complete lack of artistic skill and talent. Nevertheless he encouraged her, as it seemed to keep her happy and occupied. Besides, he no longer financially needed her working anyway.

Having passed down the hall, Brad Rotelli turned into the kitchen. He had recently had the kitchen renovated and upgraded with granite counter-tops and new stainless steel appliances. He stood for a moment admiring the handiwork of his contractors. Then he walked over to a coffee machine. Dutifully the on-board computer had already brewed his favorite variety of Columbian coffee.

Picking up the steaming hot mug of fresh-brewed coffee, Brad Rotelli walked over to a set of French doors, opened them and stepped out onto a large deck at the rear of the house. The 5,700 square foot home sat on 2.4 acres of prime real estate. As he did every morning when the weather permitted, Brad stood at the deck railing gazing out over his property. Beneath the deck was a stone patio. Beyond that was a built-in swimming pool. Beyond the swimming pool was a manicured garden whose flowers were blooming in a radiance of bright colors. Beyond the garden was a teak deck and bulkhead. Here Brad Rotelli's land property ended and the Long Island Sound began. Jutting out from this deck and bulkhead into the Sound was a fifty-foot dock. Tied alongside the right side of the dock was a 2011 forty-three-foot Four Winns Vista V-440 cabin cruiser.

To the east, the sun had risen and was bathing Long Island Sound with its radiant rays. A light breeze was blowing from the west. Small waves lapped peacefully at the bulkhead. In the distance, several boaters were out cruising the tranquil waters of the Sound. Brad Rotelli drank in the scenery and his property like he did every such morning.

Brad Rotelli finished his coffee and went back into the kitchen. Next he retrieved his leather briefcase and the keys for his 2010 black Lexus GS350 F Sport sedan from his second floor office. Then he descended a flight of stairs to the first level of his home and made his way to the front foyer.

When Brad Rotelli opened his front door to exit his home, he was surprised to see two men in dark suits standing on his front landing.

"Mr. Rotelli, we were just about to ring your door bell but you saved us the trouble," one of the men said. "Mind if we step inside and have a word with you?"

Brad Rotelli was dumbfounded by the two strange men who now stood before him. The one man's question sounded more like a command. "A word with me?" the befuddled Rotelli asked in reply.

"Mr. Rotelli, I'm Connecticut Deputy Attorney General Thomas Gearing and this is Special Agent Carl Nguyen of the Connecticut State Police," the first man said. Rotelli looked at the two men and then past them to see a dozen uniformed police officers and several men and women in business suits standing in his driveway. Marked and unmarked law enforcement vehicles were blocking his driveway.

Brad Rotelli looked back at Deputy AG Gearing. Before he could answer, Gearing spoke again.

"You're living in a $2 million waterfront home, with a $400,000 boat and two $65,000 Lexuses, and you have a half-million dollar vacation home in the Keys," said Gearing. "Did you *really* think we wouldn't notice a $110,000 a year school superintendent with all that?"

*   *   *

"We have all of your financial records. We have your co-conspirators' financial records. We have the school district's financial records. All of this proves beyond a shadow of a doubt that you conspired with your school board president, your business administrator and your district's insurance agent to defraud the Norwalk Public Schools District of $3.89 million," stated Connecticut Deputy Attorney General Thomas Gearing to Brad Rotelli and his attorney Oscar Mikoyan. They were among several attorneys gathered in a conference room in the Connecticut Attorney General's Office in Hartford. "The only question is how long you're going to prison for."

The disgraced former Superintendent of Schools for Norwalk sat with his attorney across the conference table from Gearing and two of his assistants. Rotelli's demeanor was unconcealed contempt for the man responsible for his prosecution for a host of State corruption charges. "I'm not going to prison," Rotelli angrily retorted.

"If you really believe that, you are living in a fantasy world," Gearing replied coldly. The Rotelli Case was one of several major investigations that Gearing was overseeing which involved bid rigging, bribery and other acts of government corruption. The Governor and the Attorney General had placed a high priority on combating corruption at all levels of government and Thomas Gearing was one of their star prosecutors in this effort.

Thomas Gearing was one of seven Deputy Attorney Generals that reported directly to the Attorney General. He was also head of the Attorney General's Public Corruption Task Force or CTF for short. A native of Baltimore, Maryland, he earned his undergraduate degree in finance and accounting from the University of Maryland in College Park and his law degree from Georgetown University. After graduation, he accepted a direct commission as an Ensign in the U.S. Navy's Judge Advocate General Corps, a branch of the Navy made popular by the TV series "JAG." For five years, he practiced military law, prosecuting and defending sailors and Marines who committed offenses ranging from petty theft to domestic abuse. He even had prosecuted a Navy fighter pilot for murdering a romantic rival. Following his naval service, Gearing was recruited into the Connecticut Department of Justice and worked his way up to serve as Deputy Attorney General. He was six feet tall, 180 pounds with a trim, muscular build, and short, dark hair.

The Public Corruption Task Force was a multi-agency group formed by the Attorney General specifically to target corruption in state and local government. Deputy Attorney General Gearing was the Director and Deputy Attorney General Janette Levin-Harris was the Deputy Director. The fact that the AG had assigned two of his top Deputies to serve on the CTF spoke volumes about the importance of the issue to him and the Governor. Other members of the CTF included staff attorneys, investigators from the Connecticut State Police and representatives of the Treasury Department. In addition, the CTF routinely met with the U.S. Attorney's Office to coordinate efforts to rid the state of public corruption. The relationship was most amicable with none of the turf wars and petty jealousies that one might expect between two powerful prosecutorial government agencies.

"Do you have an offer to make?" Rotelli's attorney asked.

"The AG has authorized me to offer your client a plea of fifteen years in a medium security prison with eligibility for parole at seven years and forfeiture of all his assets, taking into consideration his legal defense expenses," Gearing informed the two men. "Otherwise we'll be seeking the maximum – 25 years with no parole before 12."

Oscar Mikoyan started to say something but his client cut him off. "That's your offer?!?" Rotelli retorted incredulously. "Fifteen years?!? You're out of your freakin' mind. I'm not going to prison and you're not taking my home or anything else from me."

"It is not going to take me much effort to put you in prison for a very, very long time, Mr. Rotelli," Gearing responded. "I have a mountain of evidence against you. Your jury is going to be made up of ordinary people who are struggling to pay their mortgage, their bills and their school taxes while you're living like a prince on the Long Island Sound and vacationing at your other home in Florida. No one on your jury is going to be sympathetic to a corrupt school superintendent who defrauded his school district and the taxpayers of nearly $4 million to finance a lavish lifestyle that none of them can even hope to achieve in their lifetimes. Not a single juror is going to sympathize with you after I show them how you put your own greed ahead of their children's education and future success. All I have to do is show the jurors your pay stubs from the school district and photos of your mansions, and cars and boat and you're going to prison for bribery and corruption."

"I'm moving for a change of venue," Mikoyan interjected. "This case has already had too much publicity. My client has already been convicted in the media. He can't get fair trial anywhere near here."

"Where are you going to move the trial to, Alaska?" Gearing laughed. "It doesn't matter where we hold the trial. You're going to be convicted. Take the deal and save yourself ten years of prison time. Counselor, talk some sense into your client."

"I worked hard to get where I am and to get what I got," Rotelli snapped.

"Correction – Mr. Rotelli," Gearing interrupted. "You worked hard to steal from the taxpayers and students of Norwalk."

"I worked hard to turn that district around," Rotelli continued. His attorney tried in vain to rein in his client's outburst. "Before me, Norwalk Schools were the worst. They were consistently ranked in the bottom third of Connecticut schools in every performance category. Barely half their graduates went on to college. Their drop-out rate was the worst in our county. I turned that around. I re-built that district. The people love me in Norwalk. Now our schools are in the top ten percent of Connecticut schools in every category. Nearly 70 percent of our graduates are going on to community college or four-year colleges. Our graduation rate is one of the best in the state. I did that. *I did that!* I'm entitled to everything I've earned! And you're not going to take it away – not my home, not my boat, not my cars, none of it!"

"Be that as it may, Mr. Rotelli," Gearing answered. "You still broke the law and you're going to prison. You can either go to prison for fifteen years or twenty-five years. The choice is yours. But make no mistake, you are going to prison."

"Give me a minute to consult with my client," Mikoyan said.

"No, Oscar, I don't need a minute," Rotelli rebuffed him. "No deal."

"Well, then, I'll see you in court," Gearing answered. "Enjoy your last days of freedom." Then turning to one of his assistants, he said, "Ernesto, please show these gentlemen out."

Gearing left the conference room and headed back to his office. Along the way, he ran into Deputy Attorney General Janette Levin-Harris. "Did Rotelli take the deal?" she asked, even though she already surmised the answer.

"Of course not," Gearing answered matter of factly. "He thinks he can get off without prison time and still keep his assets. I have no sympathy for stupid, greedy people."

      *   *   *

Brad Rotelli woke up as usual at 7:15 am on the top bunk in his prison cell in Watson State Correctional Institution near the town of Belford in north-east Connecticut. He lay there for several minutes staring at the bland gray ceiling of his 10 foot by 14 foot prison cell. His cell mate, a three-time offender incarcerated for Medicare fraud, was already up and performing his morning hygiene rituals using the small stainless steel sink and toilet bolted to the concrete walls of the cell.

The disgraced former School Superintendent of the Norwalk Public Schools was thus beginning his 350th day behind bars at the Watson State Correctional Institution. After refusing a plea deal offered by the Connecticut Attorney General, Rotelli went to trial in early July 2010. During the trial which lasted five weeks, Deputy Attorney General Gearing presented a mountain of irrefutable evidence that Rotelli had received over $900,000 in bribes from insurance broker Victor Reedman between 2002 and 2009. In return, Rotelli conspired with Norwalk School Board President Lorraine Saunders and School Business Administrator Adam Franks to circumvent state school contract laws and award nearly $3 million in contracts to Reedman's insurance brokerage firm. The jury took only three hours to convict Rotelli on forty-seven counts of accepting bribes, criminal conspiracy, money laundering, income tax evasion, and violating state laws governing school contracts. He was sentenced to twenty years in prison and ordered to forfeit his two homes, his personal vehicles and his boat. His remaining assets were exhausted by his legal bills. Rotelli began serving his prison term a week after being sentenced. Reedman, Saunders and Franks took plea bargains and received prison terms ranging from three to seven years.

"Time to get up, princess," a loud voice boomed from outside the cell. Rotelli looked over to see a massive prison guard on the other side of his bars. He sat up and looked around his ten foot by 14 foot bleak prison cell. It was a far cry from his 5,700 square foot multi-million dollar waterfront mansion. All of the trappings of his former life were gone: his waterfront mansion, his vacation home, his cars and boat, etc. Even his wife was gone. Though still legally married to him, his wife out of necessity had gone back to work as a dental hygienist and was now living with a recently divorced former high school classmate.

Brad Rotelli hopped down from his bunk and walked over to the bars confining him into his narrow cell. He looked out from behind the bars. Instead of the majestic views of Long Island Sound, he saw other rows of prison cells across the corridor.

3 THE VISITOR

[Author's Note: This story contains dialogue in both English and German. The German portions are accompanied by footnotes with their English translations. If you are not familiar with the German language, then there are two ways to read this story. First, you can read the story completely through and go back and read the footnotes. Or, you can read the English translations in the footnotes as they appear in the story.]

Shortly after 6 pm on Tuesday, June 11th, 2013, there was a knock on the door of Calvin Rutledge's condominium. Calvin Rutledge was a thirty-something-year-old real estate agent living in a suburb of Sacramento, California. He was of average height and weight and had a skin complexion that defied tanning. Despite the brutal beating that the real estate market had been taking these last few years, Calvin was doing reasonably well for himself. He had a spacious yet unostentatious condominium, drove a 2011 Cooper Mini, skied regularly in Tahoe and Aspen, and had no dependents.

Calvin Rutledge had just gotten home from work when he heard that unexpected cliché knock on the door of his condo. He walked over to the door and opened it to find a man of indeterminate age, of average height and dressed in simple dark clothes standing on his front step.   "Guten tag, mein Freund," the visitor said politely. "Wie geht's heute?"[1]

Puzzled by a language he did not recognize, Calvin politely replied, "Come again?"

"Verstandst du nicht?," the visitor answered. "Ich verstande dich sehr gut."[2]

The visitor's answer did not make things any clearer for Calvin. "Is there something I can help you with?" he replied, not sure what to say.

"Ja, du kann mich helfen," the visitor replied. "Ich moechte zu kommen bitte."[3]

Without waiting for a reply, the visitor started walking towards Calvin. He was still bewildered by this bizarre conversation with a mysterious man whose language he did not understand. Calvin correctly perceived that the visitor meant him no harm and seemed to want to enter his condo. Inexplicably, though, Calvin stood aside and made no effort to hinder him. "Won't you come in," he said.

"Danke, Ich werde," the visitor said, as he casually walked by Calvin and entered into his condo.[4]

[1] Translated from German: "Good day, my friend. How are you today?"

[2] "You don't understand? I understand you very well."

[3] "Yes, you can help me. I would like to come in."

Once inside the condo, the visitor looked around the living room. "Das ist schön. Ich sehe, du bist ganz gut für sich selbst," he said.[5]

Calvin closed the front door of his condo and turned to face his uninvited guest. Oddly enough, Calvin did not feel in any danger, only a deepening sense of curiosity. "Who are you?" he asked politely.

"Wer sind ich, fragst du? Ich heisse Tod, mein Freund," the visitor answered.[6]

"Your name is Todd?" Calvin asked in reply.

"Ja, mein Name ist Tod," the visitor answered again.[7]

"Well, Todd," Calvin said, visibly pleased that at least he had a name for his mysterious guest. "What can I do for you, Todd?"

"Calvin, mein Freund ---," the visitor began.

"Wait, Todd, how do you know my name and what do you want?" Calvin said, now a little bit on edge because the visitor had addressed him by name.

---

[4] "Thank you. I will."

[5] "This is nice. I can see that you are doing quite well for yourself."

[6] "Who am I, you ask? I am called Death, my friend."

[7] "Yes, my name is Death."

"Entspannen, Calvin. Ich weiss alles über du," the visitor replied reassuringly. "Es besteht keine Notwendigkeit für Alarm."[8]

The visitor's countenance and easy manner quickly put Calvin back at ease. "Todd, I cannot understand what you are saying. What language are you speaking?" he asked.

"Ich spreche Deutsche[9]," the visitor answered.

"Dutch?" Calvin asked in reply.

"Nein, nicht Dutch, Calvin, Deutsche. Ich spreche Deutsche – die Sprache in Deutschland, Osterreich und Schweiz,[10]" the visitor patiently explained.

"Dutch, Deutsche, whatever," Calvin answered. "What is it that you want Todd?"

"Ich habe Hunger," the visitor answered. "Ich möchte einen Hamburger. Hol dir deine Autoschlüssel. Wir suchen nach einer Fahrt gehen."[11]

---

8 "Relax, Calvin. I know everything about you. There is no need for alarm."

9 "I speak German."

10 "No, not Dutch, Calvin, German. I speak German, the language of Germany, Austria and Switzerland."

11 "I am hungry. I would like a hamburger. Get your car keys. We're going for a drive."

"You're hungry and want a hamburger?" Calvin asked with sudden and apparent understanding.

The visitor nodded and replied, "Ja, ich habe Hunger und ich möchte einen Hamburger." He looked around the living room and spotted Calvin's car keys resting on a coffee table. Pointing to the keys, he said, "Holen Sie sich Ihren Autoschlüssel. Du fahrst mich zu einen Hamburger zu bekommen."[12]

Calvin looked in the direction that the visitor was pointing and quickly ascertained his meaning. "Okay, Todd, you're hungry and you want me to drive you to get a hamburger."

A look of elation came across the visitor's face. "Ja, sehr gut. Jetzt wir fahren fur einen Hamburger!"[13]

Calvin walked over to the coffee table, retrieved his keys and said, "Okay, Todd, let's go for hamburgers."

The two men quickly exited Calvin's condominium and headed out into the adjacent parking lot. Calvin located his car, clicked the keyless entry and opened the driver's door.

"Dies ist Ihr Auto?" the visitor said, laughing. "Dies ist nicht ein Auto. Dies ist ein Sarg auf Raedern! Ich bin ueberrascht, dass Sich noch am Leben sind treibende dieses Auto!"[14]

---

[12] Yes, I am hungry and I would like a hamburger. Get your car keys. You will drive me to get a hamburger."

[13] Yes, very well. Now we drive for a hamburger!"

"What? You don't like my car, Todd?" Calvin shot back, insulted by the visitor's mockery. "You can go get your own hamburger."

"Es tut mir leid, Calvin," the visitor said humbly. "Dein Auto ist sehr gut, sehr gut. Cooper Minis geben mir eine Menge von Unternehmen!"[15]

Calvin relaxed again. He did not understand the visitor's exact words but he discerned an apology somewhere in there. The two men got into the car. Calvin started up the car, backed out of the parking spot and drove to the exit of the parking lot.

Traffic was whizzing by on the busy four-lane road that ran past the condominium complex. As Calvin scanned for an opening to turn out onto the roadway, the visitor observed, "Es gibt so viel Verkehr. Wie kann man in einem solchen Verkehr zu fahren?"[16]

Calvin did not know what the visitor had said but he guessed that he was referring to the traffic. "If you think this traffic is bad, you should see morning rush hour," he said. Finally he saw an opening and darted into the eastbound lane.

For the next few minutes, Calvin headed east on the road amongst

---

[14] "Is this your car? This is not a car. This is a coffin on wheels! I am surprised that you are still alive, driving this kind of car!"

[15] "I am sorry, Calvin. Your car is very good, very good. Mini Coopers give me a lot of business."

[16] "There is so much traffic. How do you drive in such traffic?"

numerous other cars. The visitor chatted away incessantly. Calvin nodded occasionally as if he understood what his guest was saying but both of them knew that he didn't have a clue.

"Schalten Sie hier!" the visitor abruptly said, gesturing towards a restaurant on the right. "Schalten Sie hier!"[17]

"Here?! Turn here?!" Calvin said somewhat in disbelief.

"Ja, ja, schalten Sie hier!" the visitor repeated.

"Alright," Calvin said as he turned into the parking lot of a Quicky Burger restaurant. He found a parking spot near the fast food restaurant and guided the agile Cooper Mini into the spot. "Todd, if you want a hamburger, there are a lot better places than this," he observed.

"Nein, das is gut," the visitor answered. He hopped out of the car and headed into the Quicky Burger with Calvin struggling to keep up.

Quicky Burger was a not too particularly attractive low cost fast food restaurant. There were a few patrons lined up at the counter either placing orders or waiting to place orders. A few more patrons were eating in the Spartan dining area. The visitor strode up to the nearest open cashier and announced, "Guten Abend, Fraulein. Ich möchte einen Hamburger, bitte schon."[18]

---

[17] "Turn here! Turn here!"

[18] "Good Evening, Miss. I would like a hamburger, please."

The cashier was teenage girl with short brown hair and braces on her teeth. "I'm sorry. What did you say?" she asked in reply.

"Kein Grund zur Entschuldigung sein. Erhalten Sie mir bitte ein Hamburger," the visitor replied politely.[19]

Before the confused cashier could answer, Calvin walked up and stated, "You'll have to excuse my friend. He doesn't speak English. He would like a hamburger please."

The cashier's countenance changed from confusion to relief. "Okay, thank you. Would he like any fries or a drink with that?" she asked.

"Ja," the visitor said.[20]

"He'd like fries and a coke, please," Calvin said. "And I'll have the same."

"Is this for here or to go?" she asked.

"Hier," replied the visitor.[21]

"Here," replied Calvin, though his translation was not needed for this answer.

19 "No need to apologize. Just get me a hamburger, please."

20 "Yes."

21 "Here."

The cashier rang up their order, scurried around to obtain the food and beverages and presented the assembled items on a tray. "That will be $8.95 please," she said.

The visitor reached for his pocket but Calvin stopped him. "I got it, Todd," he said and handed over a ten dollar bill to the cashier.

Seconds later, she handed him back his change. "Enjoy your meal and please come again," she said with a smile.

"Danke schon," said the visitor in reply.[22]

"Thank you," said Calvin in reply.

The visitor picked up the tray and headed for the dining area with Calvin following behind. He identified a table that appeared to be reasonably clean, placed the tray on the table top and sat down. Calvin joined him at a seat across the table.

Without saying a word, the visitor dove into his hamburger and fries, periodically muttering "Sehr gut, sehr gut!"[23]

Calvin, too, began eating his gourmet fast food entrée. A smirk came across his face as he watched the elated visitor devour his hamburger. "You know, Todd, I could have taken you to a place that serves much, much better food than here," he observed in

---

[22] "Thank you very much."

[23] "Very good, very good!"

between bites.

"Das ist gut," the visitor replied. "Ich bin glücklich."[24]

In just a few minutes, the visitor had completely finished his meal and began looking impatiently at Calvin.

"You must have really been hungry," Calvin observed. Taking note of the visitor's visible restlessness, he added, "We can go whenever you like."

"Ich bin bereit jetzt gehen," answered the visitor.[25]

Calvin quickly collected the debris from his unfinished meal and picked up the tray. He got up from the table, walked over to a trash receptacle and deposited them inside. The visitor was already at the door. Calvin followed him out of the Quicky Burger and back to his car. The two re-entered Calvin's Mini Cooper.
Calvin started up the Mini and exited the parking lot onto the busy road. He made a right at the next intersection and then another right. In a few minutes, they were back at the condo complex. The whole time, the visitor sat quietly with a bemused look of contentment on his face.

Calvin pulled the Mini into his complex's parking lot and returned to the parking spot he had vacated less than half an hour before. "We're home, Todd," he informed his guest.

---

[24] "This is good. I am happy."

[25] "I am ready to go now."

The two exited the vehicle. "Are you coming inside?" Calvin asked.

The visitor shook his head. "Nein, ich muss gehen," he said with a big smile on his face. "Danke für die Hamburger."[26]

Calvin was a bit disappointed at the response. The whole experience had been quite bewildering to him but at the same time, he was quite intrigued by the mysterious visitor. "Oh, okay, Todd," he said in reply. Then he added, "Todd, who are you and why did you want me to take you for a hamburger?"

Without hesitation, the visitor answered in perfect English, "Calvin, I am Death, and sometimes, I do things that don't make any sense."

With Calvin standing there in utter shock and disbelief, Death walked off down the street and into the night.

---

[26] "No, I must be going. Thank you for the hamburger."

4   When You're Ready

"It's Mandy, are you busy? I need to talk," Mark Adams heard a familiar female voice say over his cell phone. The 22-year-old college senior was just coming out of his 10 am Constitutional Law class at Westmont University when he got the call.

"Yeah, no, I mean…yeah I can talk," Mark replied without hesitation as he descended the stairs in Owen Roberts Hall. "When?"

"Now," Mandy replied. "I'll be waiting for you at the usual place."

"Okay, see you soon." Mark ended the call. His next class was not until 12:30 pm so he could easily make some time for her. Based upon past experience, he knew why he was being summoned on such short notice.

Mark exited the academic building and strode out across the campus for the 'usual place.' The semi-wooded campus was a bustle of students heading to or from their classes. An equal number were taking advantage of the warm, sunny day in early May to lounge out, socialize and do a myriad of other non-academic activities. Of average height, build and looks, there was nothing physically that made Mark stand out from the hundreds of other college males out and about that May morning.

Westmont University was a medium-sized liberal arts college in the affluent Philadelphia suburb of Radnor, a town that also was home to much more famous Villanova University. Its mid-19th Century vintage stone academic buildings were interspersed with more modern, steel and concrete campus housing, a Student Center and administrative support buildings.

In less than a month, Mark Adams would be graduating. He had had many memorable and rewarding experiences, academic and otherwise, in his four years here. But four years was enough for him. He was ready to leave this all behind and embark upon the next phase of his life.

Barely ten minutes later, Mark caught sight of the 'usual place': a large oak tree located adjacent to a three-story modern campus apartment building that blended in surprisingly well with its surroundings. In the nearly three years that Mark had known Mandy, he had spent many hours beneath that tree with her trying to help her make sense of life.

And as expected, Mandy was beneath the tree. She was five-feet, four inches tall and dressed in a magenta Westmont University t-shirt and blue jeans. Her chestnut brown hair cascaded down her shoulders. The sight of her never failed to make Mark's pulse quicken.

21-year-old Mandy McReynolds was a junior graphics design major originally from Towson, Maryland. She and Mark had lived in this same apartment building during her sophomore year and had had several general education classes together. They quickly had become close friends. And even though nothing romantic had ever developed between them, Mandy could and did rely upon Mark to help her navigate through the perilous relationship issues that she often found herself in. Mandy possessed above average intelligence but poor judgment, especially when it came to romantic relationships. Time and time again, she came to Mark — heartbroken, confused and adrift in a sea of despair; time and time again, Mark would help her to heal her heart, bring clarity to the confusion and rescue her from despair, only to watch her repeat the cycle on the next guy that came along.

When Mark got closer, he could instantly see from Mandy's countenance that his initial instincts were correct. Her eyes were puffy. Her hair was disheveled. The emotional pain of another relationship crisis was written all over her face.

Then Mandy caught sight of Mark and her countenance changed. Her eyes lit up and a smile appeared. "Mark, I'm so glad you here," she said as he approached. Both hope and despair were in her voice. "I really need you," she said, throwing her arms around him and clutching him tightly as she had done on numerous occasions before.

"Whatever it is, you're stronger than it," Mark gently told her. "You'll survive…like you always do."

"That's only because you're here to help me," she quickly countered.

She let go of him. Tears were welling up again in her eyes.

"What happened?" Mark asked her. In his mind, there was only one explanation: her latest boyfriend had betrayed her in some way. The only question was 'how?'

"Eric slept with my little sister," she stammered out. Eric Templeton was her latest boyfriend, a junior Rugby player with a large ego, equally large trust fund, no ambition in life and a well-deserved reputation for womanizing. The little sister was Shane Brunsfeld, whom Mandy had sponsored into Gamma Delta Gamma Sorority last year. "He claimed that they were both drunk and they didn't know what they were doing. He said---"

Mark's compassion suddenly turned to anger as he bluntly interrupted her. "Dump him," he said with unusual directness. "Get rid of him. Don't have anything else to do with him." Mark had been through this scenario with Mandy a dozen or more times. She would fall for the wrong guy who take advantage of her physically and emotionally, cheat on her, and run roughshod through her emotional constitution. And then she would come to Mark looking for solace and healing.

This time was going to be different though. Mark was soon to graduate and he had had enough of collegiate relationship games. In the past, he had tried to help Mandy find the answers on her own and point her in the right direction to make the best decisions for her. Now, however, his abhorrence for the most self-gratifying instincts of the male species had been too powerful for his normally calm demeanor and diplomatic tact.

Mandy was taken aback by Mark's unusual bluntness. The tears stopped, replaced with a look of bewilderment. "Get rid of him?" she asked in reply.

"Mandy, I'm sorry for being direct but you need to get rid of him," he answered as compassionately as he could all the while struggling with his own anger at Eric. "I've seen this happen to you so many times. Eric is self-centered scumbag, no different than Jeff or Roger or all those other guys that took advantage of you. You're a beautiful person --- inside and out. And you deserve to be treated far, far better than you have been. You deserve a guy who'll love you and respect you for who you are, not use you for his own selfish reasons. If you keep falling for guys like Eric who don't love you and appreciate you, then you're just going to keep being hurt and betrayed."

Mark was even beginning to surprise himself with his bluntness. He could not be sure if he was actually getting through to her. He didn't want to be lecturing her but she needed a heavy dose of reality right now. At the same time, however, he needed to be sympathetic and compassionate.

Pausing for a few moments to let that sink in, Mark decided to return to his normal method of gentle persuasion. "Mandy, you're an amazing woman that any guy would be privileged to be with. Never forget that. Don't settle for anyone less than that."

From her countenance, Mark could tell that he had made some positive improvement in her heart. She smiled at him with much affection. "You always see things so much clearer than I," she said. Then she wrapped her arms around him again and gently whispered, "Thank you, Mark. I'd be lost without you."

It was time for Mark to head to his next class. The two parted. Mark hoped that his words would resonate within her and motivate her to change her selection criteria for men for the better.

Unfortunately, that was not the case.

*   *   *   *

Mark arrived for his next class with only a few minutes to spare and as a consequence, was forced to find a seat in the second row --- much, much closer to the front of the lecture hall than he preferred.

At exactly 12:30 pm, a short, mousy-looking middle-aged professor ambled into the lecture hall and took his usual position at a podium. "Good afternoon, scholars," Dr. Winston Almond announced to the fifty or so students gathered for his bi-weekly dose of General Psychology.   Perhaps a third of these students were here of their own free will; the remainder, like Mark, were compelled to be here by the dictates of the university's General

Education curriculum requirements. Mark had dreaded taking this class which seemed to him to be a colossal waste of his time and tuition and had thus uncharacteristically procrastinated taking it until his absolute last semester of his undergraduate career.

"Today, we are going to examine Clinical Psychology," Dr. Almond began in his customary monotone, hypnotic oral delivery, "Clinical Psychology is that branch of Psychology that studies and applies psychology to understand, prevent and relieve psychological distress, more commonly known as dysfunction, in order to promote human well-being and personal development. Today, we are going to see yet another of the marvelous ways that the study and application of psychology can and does help people to live better lives...."

After suffering through Dr. Almond's first less than enthralling lecture, Mark had decided to take this class "Pass / No Credit" --- only the second such class he had chosen to do so during his time at Welmont. He had thus far amassed a respectable B minus average on his exams and short papers with a minimal effort that would not adversely impact his strident run at Summa Cum Laude honors.

"The founding pioneer of the fascinating field of Clinical Psychology was Lightner Witmer, who served as the head of the Psychology Department at the University of Pennsylvania in the early 20th Century," Dr. Almond droned on.

But Mark's thoughts were far, far from his present locale and Dr. Almond's subject matter. Having scored a 170 out of a possible

180 points on the LSATs (Law School Admission Test), Mark had his choice of law schools. He chose Villanova University's School of Law, for its academic reputation and resources and for financial reasons. The partial tuition scholarship that he had been able to obtain would help ease the financial burden of paying for his law degree. So Mark's thoughts were on his future in law, rather than the past history of Clinical Psychology.

Abruptly though, his thoughts about law school were crowded out by another pressing issue --- his earlier conversation with Mandy. Yes, he had been rather blunt with her, perhaps even rude, but he had been with her through this cycle of romance, betrayal, despondency and recovery a dozen times. He had had enough of helping Mandy pick up the pieces of her shattered emotional state. And now he was feeling intense anger at all those guys who had trampled upon her emotionally and physically.

But at the same time, Mark held deep affections for Mandy. She was a beautiful person, even if she made abysmal relationship choices. As Dr. Almond trudged through his prepared lecture, Mark's mind recounted his past friendship with her.

Suddenly, Mark's heart took control of his mind and his right hand. He began scribbling furiously in his notebook. He filled first one page, then another with his thoughts. He reviewed them again and again. He crossed out whole lines, added new ones, crossed them out too then started writing all over again. After another review, he wrote a third draft, then a fourth draft. When he was finally satisfied with his text, he copied the words into a final draft with much better handwriting.

"And that concludes our lecture for today, class. Your final writing assignment is due next Monday. Please read Chapter 25 of your text and be prepared for a discussion." Dr. Almond's announcement came as a shock to Mark. So intent had he been on his writing that Mark had not noticed over an hour had passed. He quickly gathered his belongings and made for the door.

Dr. Almond, however, thwarted Mark's flight from the lecture hall. "Mr. Adams, something I said today must have really resonated with you," he said in an obviously pleased tone of voice. "I have never seen you so attentive in my lectures nor taking such copious notes."

Mark was for a moment at a loss for words but soon found them. "Yes, your lecture was very thought provoking," he offered.

"Excellent!" the professor replied jubilantly. "Enjoy the rest of your day and see you next class!"

*   *   *   *

After Mark had left her by the tree, Mandy returned to her apartment. She mulled over Mark's advice for a while. Despite his unusual harshness, Mandy knew that Mark had her best interests in mind. But Mark did not know Eric the way that she did. Eric was different from the others, she told herself. He would not intentionally hurt her. It was all a big, unfortunate misunderstanding.

Her mind made up, Mandy called Eric on his cell phone. Getting his voice-mail instead, she tried his room at his fraternity house. Much to her horror, Shane answered the phone. Unable to speak, she quickly hung up the phone and spent the remainder of the afternoon sobbing on her bed. Her phone rang several times but she ignored it each time, preferring instead the solitude of her own misery.

*   *   *   *

Mark had another class in the afternoon. He had wanted to rush over to Mandy's apartment, but resisted the urge. Knowing her schedule, he knew that he would not find her there until at least 8 p.m. Nor was he inclined to try and track her down. What he had to do had to be done in private.

Had he known that Mandy had spent the entire afternoon in her apartment in her latest morass of misery, Mark would have come by much, much earlier.

At a few minutes after 8 p.m., there was a knock on Mandy's door. Her first instinct was that it might be Eric. She wiped the tears from her eyes and headed for her door.

The door opened and Mandy appeared. Instantly, Mark knew that she had not followed his sage advice and dumped Eric and now it appeared that the situation had worsened. This time, however, he was not here to console her.

"Mark, I'm so glad you're here," Mandy said with a look of relief on her face.

Mark replied in a soothing voice, "Listen, Mandy, I can't stay but I need to give you this."   He handed over a plain white letter-sized envelope.

Mandy now looked puzzled as she accepted the envelope. "But Mark I really need you, Eric…"

"I'm sorry but I can't stay," he interrupted. Before she could protest, he was gone.

Mandy closed the door. Still puzzled by the abruptness of Mark's visit, she opened the envelope and began reading.

After a few seconds she gasped, then slumped to the floor and leaned back across the now closed apartment door. Tears began welling up in her eyes.

She read the letter a second time, then a third time and a fourth time. Finally, she broke down in uncontrollable sobs and buried her face in her hands.

*   *   *   *

Mark graduated from Westmont University with a Bachelors of Arts in Political Science and matriculated at Villanova University School of Law that fall. Three years later, he graduated from there with a Juris Doctor degree, specializing in real estate law. He immediately went to work for the law firm of Stratford and Hughes located in Center City, Philadelphia.

Eight years after graduating from Westmont, Mark Adams was a rising star in the Philadelphia legal community. He had quickly established an enviable reputation for legal knowledge, sound judgment and integrity. He was on the fast track to make partner at Stratford and Hughes and had already earned enough to pay off his law school debts.

Mark Adams represented a wide variety of clients requiring aid in real estate matters. Though initially starting with large corporate clients, the partners at his firm soon realized that Mark had a unique repertoire with small business owners and private individuals --- people with far greater personal stake in the real estate matter at hand than a corporate CEO or Board of Shareholders. So they re-assigned him to handle those clients and were gratified by the results. Mark treated each client as if he/she were his only client, regardless of the client's financial resources, and social standing. Since most of Stratford and Hughes's clients were financially well off, Mark's billable hours were generating much revenue for his firm.

The key to Mark's repertoire with his clients was his inherent goodness, his idealism and, oddly enough, his disdain for the legal profession. In his mind, the law was made overly complicated by attorneys and politicians intentionally crafting the law as such so as to establish a legal oligarchy removed from the general populace.

To emphasize his disdain for legal professionals, Mark had hung on the wall behind his oak desk a matted frame bearing words written about lawyers by the famed Christian Humanist Desiderius

Erasmus in his *In Praise of Folly*:

> And among them our advocates challenge the first place, nor is there any sort of people that please themselves like them: for while they daily roll Sisyphus his stone, and quote you a thousand cases, as it were, in a breath no matter how little to the purpose, and heap glosses upon glosses, and opinions on the neck of opinions, they bring it at last to this pass, that that study of all other seems the most difficult.

These words never failed to have an effect. A few fellow attorneys found the quote amusing; most were offended at this biting criticism of their profession, which was exactly what Mark intended by their placement.

Though he did enjoy the financial rewards of his success, Mark's true motive for entering the law thus was to reform it from within. He found the law to be overcomplicated and unnecessarily beyond the comprehension of most ordinary citizens. His intent, thus, was to make the bewildering complexities of the law understandable to people who had not dropped six figures to earn a law degree. And he was very good at doing so.

Mark Adams arrived at his office in Center City at his usual 7:30 am and immediately plunged into his work. He spent his first hour reviewing real estate contracts. From 8:30 am to 10 am, he attended the weekly staff meeting for Stratford and Hughes's Real Estate Division. From 10 am until 12 pm, he wrote pre-trial motions and conducted legal research. He left the office for an hour to grab lunch, then returned for the first of his three afternoon meetings with clients.

At 2:25 p.m., one of the secretaries called him on the intercom, "Mr. Adams, your two-thirty appointment is here."

Mark looked again at his calendar: 2:30 p.m. Abigail Goodwin. He did not recognize the name nor did he have any information on her case except a brief line that stated "Real Estate Transaction."

"Send her in, please, Stephanie," Mark replied.

Shortly thereafter, the door to his office opened and in walked a five-foot, four-inch tall woman in her late 20s, wearing business attire. Her chestnut brown hair was tied up in a bun. "Hello, Mark, it's been a long time," she said.

"I'm sorry, Mandy, that I did not recognize your new name," Mark apologized as he stood up and came around his desk to greet her. His pulse quickened again at the sight of this ghost from his past suddenly materializing in front of his eyes.

Mandy and Mark briefly shook hands and he showed her to leather chair in front of his desk. Then he returned to his chair behind his desk and grabbed a legal pad. A quick glance of disapproval from Mandy and a subtle shaking of her head indicated that she was not ready for formal business yet; so Mark put down his pen. Then he noticed that there weren't any rings on her left hand.

Mark was rapidly processing new information about Mandy from her appearance and integrating it into what he already knew. The name change and the lack of corresponding rings indicated two possibilities to him; she was either divorced or in the process of getting a divorce.

Mandy, too, was assessing her surroundings. Mark's office was adorned with certificates and diplomas testifying to his legal prowess. Other frames held photos of various places that he had visited. Without saying it, Mandy noted with relief that Mark's office was devoid of any photos indicating an ongoing romantic relationship of any kind; similarly, his left hand was also devoid of any rings.

"I'm sorry that we've lost touch all these years," she began hesitatingly, "but I need your help."

It had been eight years actually. The two had not spoken since Mark had delivered his handwritten note to Mandy at her apartment on the day she discovered Eric Templeton had slept with her little sister in Gamma Delta Gamma.

Mark was about to say something in reply but caught himself when he realized she was not finished.

"I've made a mess of my life," she continued. "I should have listened to you when you told me to dump Eric and stop letting guys use me. I have had a series of disastrous relationships that led up to me marrying the wrong guy for the wrong reasons. Three years ago, I met a guy in Cancun, Hamilton Goodwin. He's from Philly. We moved in together a few weeks later and got married the following year.   His family is loaded and so he really doesn't work, even though he's got a stock broker license. He married me just to get his parents off his back about him being single and I married him because I didn't want to keep hopping from relationship to relationship and I didn't want to be alone. But being married to him was far worse than being alone. Mentally, he's still a frat boy and he acts like it. He parties and drinks and hooks up. He's cheated on me at least a dozen times that I know of and probably a lot more that I don't.   I finally reached my breaking point and walked out on him."

Mark sat spellbound at Mandy's revelations.   He was struck, however, by her demeanor. This was not the usual Mandy coming to him in tears, devastated by her latest relationship disaster. Though her eyes were moist with emotion, the Mandy before him was much more in control of herself. Her description of her recent travails was circumspect. Mark was gladdened that she had gained much maturity in the intervening years but saddened at the same time that it had come at such a high emotional and psychological price.

"If you need a divorce attorney, I can recommend several friends and colleagues here in our firm," he offered when she paused. "I'm afraid, though, that divorce is not my area of expertise, otherwise I would do whatever I could to help you."

"I know you would, Mark," she replied. "And I appreciate your concern. You were always such a great friend in college, so supportive and understanding." She paused, took a breath, then continued, "The divorce was finalized three weeks ago. I'll be changing my name back to McReynolds soon. His parents made us sign a pre-nup and like a fool, I went along with it, so the divorce was rather simple. I got only what I brought into the marriage and nothing more, except a pitiful alimony settlement."

"I truly am sorry that things didn't work out for you. Do you need a place to stay?" Mark asked, sympathetically. "Real estate is my area of expertise. I have lots of connections. I can have you in a new place tonight if you want."

"No, I have an apartment," she answered. Then reading his mind as to her reason for being here today, she added, "I just came by today to give you this…" She reached into her pocket book and pulled out a small, plain envelope. She handed it over and got up to leave. "It was great to see you again but I have to go now."

And before Mark could intervene, she was gone.

Mark sat for several minutes trying to make sense of what had just happened in his office. After not seeing her or talking to her for eight years, Mandy showed up out of the blue, shared with him the painful details of her failed marriage and then just as unexpectedly fled his office without asking for any help in putting her life back together like she had so many times before in college.

Then Mark remembered the envelope Mandy had handed him before she left. He opened the envelope and pulled out a handwritten letter that he instantly recognized. The paper was well-worn, no doubt from countless times of being handled. There were dry tear stains, which had caused the ink to smear a little in several places.

Then Mark began to read the lines that he had written eight years previously while suffering through that dreadful General Psychology class…

May 1, 2004

Dearest Mandy,

For two years, I have watched you suffer through a succession of failed relationships that always end up with you hurt and me helping you to pick up the pieces of your broken heart. It breaks my own heart to watch other guys repeatedly trample on your heart, betray your trust and use you for their own selfish needs. You deserve better than that. You have so much to offer the right guy, yet time after time you give your heart away to guys who are unworthy of that great treasure. I have tried so many times to help you see what a special woman you are. I can no longer watch other guys break your heart. I can no longer help you trying to heal from another betrayal. You are far too beautiful a person to be treated the way that Eric and those other guys like him have been treating you. When you are ready for a man who will love you as you deserve to be loved, give me a call.

Love Always,

Mark

As Mark read those words which he had written so long ago, that scene outside her apartment came flooding back in a torrent of memories. Then he noticed that Mandy had written something at the bottom…

June 12, 2012

Dearest Mark,

I'm ready. If you still mean what you wrote back then, meet me at the usual place tonight at 8.

Mandy

*   *   *   *   *

For the first time since graduating, Abigail McReynolds walked on to the campus of Westmont University around 7:15 pm.   In her note, she had told Mark to meet her at 8; a need to collect her thoughts caused her to arrive earlier than that.

Professionally, Mandy had had a moderately successful career as a graphic artist. She had no trouble finding employment after graduation and had changed firms twice when offered more lucrative compensation packages. Personally, her life had gotten worse with a succession of failed relationships, culminating in a disastrous marriage to a philandering over-age frat boy with a trust fund and no sense of personal or financial responsibility.

As she walked around campus, Mandy replayed in her mind every bad relationship decision she had ever made, trying to learn from them in the hopes of never repeating them. A thousand doubts and self-recriminations flooded through her mind. All through college, the man she was seeking was right beside her, yet she could not recognize him for who he truly was. She could not see that the gentle compassion he offered her time after time was really a deep heartfelt expression of love for her. Why couldn't she see that? Why had she fallen for so many guys who just wanted to use her physically? How could she have been so stupid, so naïve, so blind to reality?

At another time, she would have succumbed under the bombardment of these doubts and self-recriminations. Personal growth produced by painful experience had sufficiently fortified her psyche to withstand this onslaught. She reviewed this succession of disastrous episodes in her life with a maturity and introspection that she had not previously possessed.

Fifteen minutes before 8 o'clock, Mandy positioned herself underneath the large oak tree that still stood outside her former apartment building. She remembered all the hours she had spent with Mark on this spot, all the times she had poured out her heart to him and all the times he had so lovingly consoled her. Her mind was a whirl of emotions and thoughts. However, she was able to maintain a certain level of calm and control. Yes, she regretted deeply not having realized Mark's love for her sooner and for all the time and emotion she had wasted on other guys. Yes, she feared that her realization had come too late and that he would not still love her today like he had done so many years ago. But her mind and heart were comforted by a guarded optimism that perhaps he might still love her in spite of the time and distance which had separated their two last meetings.

The minutes ticked by agonizingly slow. She successfully fought off her growing anxieties and fears.

At eight o'clock, Mark had not shown up. Mandy did not take this as a good omen; Mark was punctual to a fault.

At fifteen minutes past eight, Mark still had not shown up. Her optimism was waning. It was becoming more likely that whatever Mark had felt for her in college had faded with time and she had only herself to blame.

After waiting for thirty minutes, Mandy reluctantly but realistically reached the conclusion that she had lost her one opportunity for love and happiness with Mark. She was very disappointed in herself but made the conscious choice not to dwell on her past mistakes any longer. The next time that the right man appeared in her life, she would not forsake that opportunity. Even if Mark did not show tonight, even if she had wasted so much time and emotion on the wrong guys when she should have been with Mark, even if she had not fully experienced Mark's love as she should have, that his love had ultimately benefited her by helping her to see the beauty of her soul, her self-worth, and her dignity as a woman.

As she started to walk away from the usual place beneath the large oak tree and with it her past relationship failings, Mandy suddenly she heard a voice from the past whisper her name. She turned to find Mark standing behind her, his face aglow with a warm smile.

Somehow he had managed to sneak up on her unnoticed. "I stopped to get these for you," he said, producing a bouquet of red roses. "Sorry I kept you waiting."

"I should be the one apologizing, Mark, for keeping you waiting all these years. I wasted so much time on other guys when I should have been with you all along," Mandy said, remorse heavy in her voice. "I ----"

Mark interrupted her: "Enough said, Mandy. The past is past. Our future awaits." Then he kissed her.

5 HOME TO GLENALLEN

It was a two hour drive from Austin-Bergstrom International Airport in the city of Austin, Texas to Glenallen, Texas. After retrieving his luggage, Mike McBride got a rental car and started driving. The two-hour drive itself was not all that difficult for Mike McBride who was used to driving long distances; it was the journey there that was the challenge.

Glenallen was a small town in the Texas Hill Country numbering some 1,100 or so persons according to the 2010 U.S. Census. The town had been founded in 1866 by two brothers, Glen and Allen Smyth. Originally from the Shenandoah Valley of Virginia, the Smyth brothers and a few others who had fought on the losing side of the Civil War left their native state and headed west to start new lives. Like most of the other first families of Glenallen, the Smyth brothers were descended from the Scotch-Irish who first settled in the Valley.

If you were from Glenallen, Texas, there was one of three things you did after graduating from high school. You farmed. You worked for a business that was somehow connected with farming. Or you got the hell out of Glenallen. That's what Mike McBride had done ten years ago…and never looked back.

Mike never judged or looked down on those who had stayed behind, but he never once regretted or second-guessed leaving Glenallen.

Even before graduating from high school, Mike McBride had his exit strategy in place. In February of his senior year, he had enlisted in the U.S. Marine Corps through the Delayed Entry Program. Three days after graduating, McBride left for Marine Corps Recruit Depot San Diego, California for "Boot Camp."

There was only one thing that was keeping McBride in Glenallen. Leaving her wasn't easy…but not impossible.

The athletic McBride had done well in Boot Camp, graduating towards the top of his class, then traveled up to Marine Corps Base Camp Pendleton for Marine Corps Training, where he went through the standard infantry training that all non-infantry Marines go through before heading to their respective MOS (Military Occupational Specialty) schools. After MCT, McBride went to Fort Leonard Wood, Missouri to attend the Marine Corps's

Engineer School at Marine Corps Base Camp Lejeune in North Carolina. Following graduation from Engineer School, McBride returned to the West Coast and was assigned to Marine Wing Support Squadron 373. Later, he served with 1st Marine Division and 1st Marine Logistics Group, both of which were at Camp Pendleton. In the succeeding years, he was steadily promoted and did a tour in Iraq and a deployment aboard ship with Marine Expeditionary Unit 11 to the Western Pacific.

Now, Staff Sergeant Mike McBride was heading home to Glenallen, Texas, for the first time in ten years. His father had passed away suddenly a few years ago from an early heart attack. Mike missed the funeral because he was participating in training exercise in South Korea. His mom had subsequently remarried and moved to Killeen. His older sister before him had left Glenallen and was married and living in Fort Worth. His younger sister had left Glenallen with their mother and new step-father.

As McBride's rental car drove him closer and closer to Glenallen, the memories of his former life became more and more vivid. Eventually, he reached his exit and got off the Interstate heading east. Another twenty minutes on a county road later and McBride crossed into the corporate limits of Glenallen. Along the way, more and more familiar sights greeted him. He slowed when he approached a seemingly ordinary farm road that shot off into a cornfield. That was where he and Kara had their first kiss...in the front seat of his hand me down Ford truck.

Continuing on, he turned off the county road and snaked through a few side streets until he came to a ranch-style one-story house with a front porch and several large oak trees scattered around the property. The new owners had changed a few things but essentially the house looked the same as when Kara had lived there with her family. McBride had heard that Kara's parents had divorced six or seven years ago and sold the house.

McBride returned to the county road and set off for the next stop on his journey into the past. Glenallen High School was located about a ten minute drive from Kara's former family home. The high school was a two-story brick building built in the 1920s when the town was doing well financially and needed a high school to accommodate its growing population. McBride played sports but wasn't a star athlete. It being Saturday, school was not in session, so he drove around the back of the school and parked near the football field. He did not get out but he could see everything he needed to see from the front seat of his rental car. The football field looked like any other high school football field in Texas: goal posts, sod painted with yard lines and numbers, field lighting on eighty foot high wooden poles, a steel and wood bleacher structure topped with an announcer's booth. McBride looked out on the field that he never played on (baseball was his sport) and could see Kara with her pom-poms cheering on the sidelines.

While they were dating, Mike had attended every football game not to support his high school team but because his girlfriend was on the cheerleading squad at the game. Then his attention turned to the bleachers. On countless occasions, Mike and Kara had snuck out of class to meet underneath those bleachers. From there, he could also see the outside entrance to the high school gym. He had attended his senior prom and her junior prom in that gym. Looking at the entrance, he could see her in a magenta prom dress that took his breath away and stood in stark contrast to his beat up truck that brought them there.

Having spent ten minutes or so immersed in his high school memories, Mike got his car moving again and exited the high school grounds. Glancing at the clock on the car's radio, Mike decided to forego several other places he had wanted to swing by and head directly to his ultimate destination.

Growing up in a small town, Kara and Mike and their respective families had known each other their whole lives. Mike's older sister and Kara's older brother both had dated in high school but nothing ever came of it. Their families attended the same church, the Glenallen Presbyterian Church. She was a year younger than him. It was not until Mike's junior year and Kara's sophomore that the two tried dating and quickly found a deep emotional relationship. All that ended when he left for the Marine Corps. They both wanted different things out of life and so there was no animosity over the break-up. It was just one of things that happened when distance intruded on a relationship.

Mike tried not to think about what his life might have been if he had stayed in Glenallen and married Kara. They had taken different roads and he had not regretted it.

Ten minutes later, Mike turned his car into the Oak Grove Cemetery. There were a lot of cars parked around the cemetery which dated back to the 1880s. A hearse was parked at the head of a funeral procession. Twenty yards away a small canopy for the family of the deceased was set up amidst headstones. A crowd of people was forming around the casket that had been placed for the graveside ceremony.

Along the curb, at least fifty Patriot Guard Riders were standing in line holding large American flags. They were a volunteer organization that had been founded in 2005 in response to a radical group which was protesting at the funerals of American service members who had died in Iraq and Afghanistan. Their mission was to shield the families from the protesters. Fortunately, no protesters showed up to disrupt the funeral.

As Mike scanned around for a place to park, he said aloud, "I think the whole county is here."
With some difficulty, Mike found a spot to park his rental car.

Kara, too, had left Glenallen after graduating from high school. A gifted student, Kara had earned an academic scholarship to Texas A&M University. She also joined the Texas Army National Guard to help further finance her education. At Texas A&M, she pursued a degree in civil engineering. After graduation, the National Guard commissioned her as a second lieutenant. Unlike Mike, Kara returned to Glenallen. She got a job with the County Engineering Department and continued to serve in the National Guard.

Mike had had a number of first experiences with Kara. She would always occupy a special place in his heart, a place that could not be replaced by his wife Jill or their two young daughters. Kara was Mike's past; Jill and the girls were his present and his future. He could not imagine his life without them.

Mike got out of his rental car. He was dressed in his Marine Corps blue dress uniform adorned with the medals and ribbons he had earned during ten years of service. He walked around to the passenger side of the car and opened the door for Jill. Also dressed in a Marine Corps blue dress uniform, Sergeant Jill Hayes-McBride had hardly said a word during the drive. She knew her husband was dealing with some difficult emotions and respectfully was giving him the silence he needed to process them. Periodically, her mother would text her with updates and photos on how the girls were doing back in California.

Jill emerged from the rental car. She grasped his left arm to physically convey her love and support to him in this difficult moment. They walked together towards the gathering crowd. When they approached the line of Patriot Guard Riders, several words of support and appreciation were voiced to them. A middle-aged man wearing a black leather jacket emblazoned with the POW/MIA logo step aside to let them pass and offered "Thank you for your service, Devil Dogs." Jill smiled in return and mouthed the words, "Thank you too."

Just past the Patriot Guard Line, one of Mike's former classmates spotted him and came over. "Mike, I was hoping that you'd come," Steve Keogh said. "I know my aunt and uncle will appreciate you coming and paying your respects."

Mike nodded an acknowledgement and he and Jill continued on. Several other people noticed Mike and offered muted greetings. He and Jill positioned themselves where they could see a casket draped with an American flag. A short distance away, an honor guard of soldiers in dress uniforms with rifles stood at attention. Mike and Jill knew the routine. This was not the first military funeral that they had attended.

Near the casket stood a man Mike recognized – the Reverend William McDade, Pastor of the Glenallen Presbyterian Church –

and another face he did not recognize – a U.S. Army chaplain in dress uniform.

"On behalf of the O'Neil Family, I thank you for joining us today," said Rev. McDade in his booming voice that usually echoed off the walls of his church on Sunday mornings. "I thank you for joining with us as we say our last good-bye to our dear sister in Christ and friend, Kara O'Neil, who gave her life for our freedom in Afghanistan.   I knew Kara from the time she was born and watched with pride how she grew up to be an exemplary Christian, young woman and Army officer. We are all profoundly saddened by her leaving us so soon. We feel anger that she was taken from us by a Taliban IED while she was working so hard to help the people of Afghanistan build a new future. But we are also filled with the comfort of faith, faith in a loving and merciful God with whom Kara is now spending eternity and the hope that we, her brothers and sisters in Christ, will someday be reunited with her in God's Kingdom....."

The graveside committal proceeded according to the well-established protocols and traditions. At their conclusion, the honor guard presented arms, and fired several salutes while another soldier played the mournful strains of "Taps."

6 THE VERTIGO PROJECT

Agent Balck crept stealthily down a darkened alley in a seedy section of south Dublin. Despite the late hour, there were still a few late night revelers wandering aimlessly through the streets, hence Balck's preference for the darkened alley that he was stealthily creeping down in a seedy section of south Dublin at present. His standard issue 10mm Sig Sauer pistol clutched in his left hand, Balck's covert operative skills and senses were on high alert, ready for any contingency that might arise in the life and death struggle that was international espionage. His orders had been brief, concise and explicit: obtain a mocha latte, no cream, one sugar by any means necessary, and if he had time, discover what was the Vertigo Project – a mysterious project currently being undertaken by Russian Foreign Intelligence Service that had been baffling the American Central Intelligence Agency's most intelligent minds since the beginning of this paragraph.

Suddenly he heard the distinctive metallic click of a hammer of a 17th Century French Marin le Bourgeoys .68 caliber flintlock dueling pistol being cocked into firing position behind him. He spun around to find himself staring into the barrel of the deadly black powder pistol which had been modified to accept a silencer. "Hands in the air, slowly," said a raspy voice in English with a Norwegian accent.

"Sourdough, I should have known it was you," Balck replied as he complied with the command. Sven Sourdough was an enforcer and hired assassin for the People's Liberation Army of Downtown Oslo (PLADO), one of Norway's most notorious terrorist organizations. "Who sent you?" Balck demanded.

"People who really don't care for you," Sourdough replied.

"Well, that narrows it down," Balck retorted wryly.

"I shall now have the long awaited satisfaction of watching a sixty-eight caliber lead ball tear through your flesh and end your irritating life," Sourdough said as he squeezed the trigger.

Balck braced himself for the expected bullet. But nothing happened. All he heard was a metallic clink as the hammer struck the pan.

"Ha!" Balck retorted. "Why do you use that relic?" he sneered sarcastically. "That belongs in a museum, not in the hands of a supposedly trained assassin."

As Sourdough fiddled with the antique firearm, Balck brought his own pistol into firing position and took deliberate aim.

Suddenly, there was a flash of flame, a cloud of smoke and a muffled explosion as the flintlock pistol finally fired its lead ball. The ball ricocheted off the wall harmlessly.

Balck was momentarily blinded by the flash and smoke. When his eyesight returned, he was alone in the alley. Sourdough had escaped yet again.

* * *

His name was Edward Balck, codenamed Flashdance. Apparently someone in the Agency's Bureau of Code Names (BCN for short) didn't really like him and so stuck him with the title of a 1980s dance movie.

Balck had just finished his second burrito when the waitress brought over a third burrito, then a fourth and a fifth. By now Balck felt like he was going to explode from all the meat, cheese and beans he had consumed. Yet he was no closer to discovering the truth about the Vertigo Project than when he had entered the Mexican – Micronesian fusion restaurant known as El Something or Other three hours before.

Balck was just paying his tab when a mysterious figure entered the restaurant that he immediately recognized as Agent Care Bear. "Flashdance, join me for a burrito," he said.

"No, I just had a five," Balck answered. "I couldn't possibly eat any more."

"That wasn't an invitation," Care Bear replied as he pulled out a sawed off blunderbuss from beneath his jacket. He motioned Balck to an empty booth.

The two men quickly sat down. "Balck now realized that his new dinner companion was not Agent Care Bear but one of Care Bear's identical triplet siblings, Agent Evil Twin," Balck said to no one in particular. "Both Care Bear and Evil Twin had entered the clandestine service together; their third identical sibling decided to become a used car salesman and had a lucrative dealership outside of Fresno, California that specialized in late model French sedans. But after entering clandestine service, Evil Twin had gone rogue. He bounced around from city to city, country to country, continent to continent, offering his services to the highest bidder. The question was…who was Evil Twin working for today?"

"I don't need a history lesson," Evil Twin angrily snapped. "I know who I am."

"Yeah, but the readers don't," Balck answered.

"Fine," Evil Twin agreed. "But the readers also should know what a bunch of morons are running the CIA. After all, they hired a guy named 'Evil Twin' into clandestine service. With a name like 'Evil Twin,' how did they not see that I would go rogue someday?"

Evil Twin let that question hang ominously in the air, then remembered what he was doing there. He leveled the sawed off blunderbuss at Balck. "Prepare to meet your maker Flashdance."

The hammer struck the pan, sparks flew and a large puff of white smoke appeared but no shot was fired. "Damn," Evil Twin growled. "The powder must have gotten wet when I ran the blunderbuss through the dishwasher."

"Now, who's the moron, Evil Twin?" Agent Flashdance observed.

There was no answer. The booth was engulfed with smoke. When the smoke cleared, Evil Twin and his malfunctioning blunderbuss were nowhere to be seen.

Then something caught Flashdance's eye. He spied a small card lying on the ground. He reached down and picked it up. He carefully read the writing on the card: "The bearer is entitled to one Complimentary Espresso Dark at the Red Square Starbucks, Moscow." Handwritten on a line beneath those words was the name "Evil Twin."

"So, I must be getting close to discovering what the Vertigo Project is if the Russians are sending Evil Twin to kill me," he said to three drunk tourists who happened to have stumbled into the alley by mistaken.

* * *

The time was just before 3 am when Agent Flashdance, aka Edward Balck, reported in at the CIA Safe House, a pub frequented by CIA agents across the street from the U.S. Embassy in Dublin. He was there to meet the CIA Station Chief, codenamed Station Chief, to update him on the progress of his investigation into the Vertigo Project.

The Station Chief was seated in his usual corner booth surrounded by several unopened bottles of dishwasher detergent and a half-eaten blueberry pie. "I heard you've had quite an exciting night," Station Chief observed.

"That's for certain," Flashdance answered as he slid into the seat across from his boss. "I survived two assassination attempts and five burritos at El Something or Other. I know I must be getting close to discovering what the Vertigo Project is. That must be why the Russians sent Evil Twin to kill me."

"Indeed," Station Chief agreed. "There's been a development in the case. That's why I had you meet me here at this odd hour."

Agent Flashdance gave his boss a puzzled, scrutinizing look.

"I'm taking you off the case," Station Chief continued. "Apparently, the author has lost interest in writing this story and is pulling the plug on......"

7 Nadia

She was the most gorgeous woman that he had ever seen in his twenty years of life. Standing five feet, eight inches tall with long flowing flaxen hair and an olive complexion no doubt the result of many hours spent in the sun, she was the embodiment of the fabled California blonde. He was instantly captivated from the first moment he laid eyes upon this stunning nubile young American woman. Her mere appearance unleashed in him a nearly uncontrollable carnal lust for her that he had never known before.

Oddly enough, the object of his obsession demonstrated a surprising interest in him as well. She had in fact approached him that fateful day a month ago when they had first met. He was sitting by himself at an outdoor table in the International Plaza in front of the University of Southern California's Ronald Tutor Campus Center. He saw her from across the plaza. She soon caught notice of him gawking at her, but rather than be repulsed or unnerved by his unconcealed, even creepy, attention, she came over to him and began a conversation with him. From this encounter, a passionate relationship was starting to develop, albeit not as quickly as he would have liked.

Her attraction to him and the resultant budding relationship was most unusual as she was unquestionably in a completely different social realm than the socially awkward freshman chemistry student from the city of Khan Yunis in the Gaza Strip. Whereas she was tall and attractive with an exquisite figure, Ahmed was short with a body, limbs and a head all out of proportion to each other. Her face could melt the heart of any man; his face was so ordinary and unremarkable that it could melt into any multi-cultural crowd.

Only four months ago, he had only moved to the U.S. to attend USC and was still adjusting to his new environs. To say that it was a culture shock would be a massive understatement. His father was a minor official in the city government which placed him and his family in the small middle class of the Hamas state. Though better off than most Palestinians, Ahmed's world was still wrought with the poverty, high unemployment, political unrest and hatred for Israel symptomatic of the Gaza Strip. He struggled psychologically with the opulence and decadence of southern California which stood in such stark contrast with the impoverished hopelessness of his homeland. Ever mindful of the plight of his people back home, he would not succumb to the decadence of America. He would dedicate himself to learning and acquiring the knowledge and skills to empower his people and lift them up from their debasement. He would return to his homeland and continue the struggle for his people. He would not be seduced by the materialism, wealth, and hedonism of his current surroundings.

That was his original intent. Of course, fate and voluptuous femininity had intervened in a most dramatic fashion. Now he sat here again at a table on the International Plaza contemplating his life and his obsessive desires for her. He had to have her, to possess her. Their relationship was not progressing physically as quickly as he wanted. Despite the forwardness of her initial meeting with him, she was more conservative in the progression of the physical aspects of their relationship. Ahmed, burning with intense desire for this ravishing enchantress, did not know how much longer he could wait for her "to be ready" to take their relationship to the next level.

Then suddenly she was there, sliding into a seat next to him at the table. "Good morning Ahmed, I only have a few moments before my next class but I wanted you to have them," she said almost apologetically.

"Nadia, I need more than a few moments with you," Ahmed replied. "I need to see you tonight. I need you."

"Ahmed, I have been thinking a lot about us," Nadia said softly. "You mean so much to me and you have been sooo very patient with me. From the first day I met you, I was drawn to you but I needed time to sort things out, to understand what I was feeling for you." She paused, trying to discern his thoughts from his countenance. She was astute enough to know social and cultural norms in his homeland were very different than hers.

A look of puzzlement presently appeared on his face which was quickly followed by one of frustration. She carefully weighed her next words. "Ahmed, what I am trying to say is that I did not want to rush into anything with you," she said softly. "And you have been so patient with me." She paused again and took a deep breath. "I think I am ready. Tonight, I think I am ready to be with you."

A deluge of lustful desire swept over Ahmed. *"At last!"* he thought *"At last you will be mine! Tonight you will be mine!"*

But while thoughts of sexual conquest flooded through his mind and body, Ahmed was careful to suppress them outwardly. He smiled with reserve. "Nadia, I understand your hesitation and if you are not ready, we can wait," he answered disingenuously.

Nadia looked intently into Ahmed's eyes for a few long moments. "Tonight, my love," she finally replied. "Tonight, I will ready for you."

*   *   *   *

The rest of the day passed agonizingly slow for Ahmed. Though he was physically in his classes, his mind was overwhelmed by the prospects of having Nadia later that night. He felt as if his mortal body could not contain his desires for her.

Around 9 pm, there was a knock on the door of Ahmed's off-campus apartment. Stressing the importance of this night, he had prevailed upon his roommate to spend the night elsewhere so that he could be alone with Nadia for this consequential moment in their relationship. Ahmed answered the door and saw her standing in the hallway.

Nadia was dressed in gym shorts and a t-shirt. Her luxurious blonde hair was hidden underneath a LA Dodgers baseball cap. Over her right shoulder, she had slung a backpack typical of a college student. Ahmed could not care in the least how she was dressed. All that mattered to him was what was underneath those clothes.

Ahmed beckoned Nadia to come, then closed the door behind her and secured all of its locks. She embraced him and kissed him passionately in a way that she had never done before. "Let's not waste any more time," she said coyly. She gently pulled away from him and headed for the bathroom. "I'll meet you in your bedroom. Be ready for a night like you've never experienced before."

Ahmed watched the bathroom door close, then rushed into his bedroom. His heart was pounding. His testosterone levels and libido were skyrocketing as he stripped down to his underwear. Impatiently he waited for her next to his bed.

A few minutes later, Nadia entered his bedroom wearing a pink silk robe that ended half-way down her thighs. She still had her backpack on her shoulder. She closed the bedroom door behind her, then turned back to him. He started to say something but she cut him off by shoving him backwards onto his bed. He was both startled and aroused by her aggressiveness. "If we're going to do this…," she said seductively. "We're going to do this *my way*."

Ahmed was dumbfounded but nevertheless undeterred in his desire for her. He meekly nodded in acquiescence. Nadia placed the backpack on the edge of the bed and retrieved several short lengths of rope from it. Again, Ahmed started to speak but Nadia repeated, "We're doing this myyyyyy way."

Nadia quickly tied Ahmed's feet to the footboard at the end of his bed. "I know that you are a man of the world, Ahmed," she said as she tightened the ropes around his ankles. "But here in America, we like to play rough sometimes."

In all of his fantasies about this night, this particular scenario which was rapidly evolving had never once entered into his thoughts. He was always the one acting aggressively and forceful, yet Nadia had completely taken control. His shock at the unexpected role reversal was overcome by his lustful desire for her. He would have her…even if it meant playing by her rules.

Nadia then tied Ahmed's wrists to the headboard of his bed. He was completely outstretched and vulnerable, yet he was still overwhelmed by lust and desire. Surprisingly he found himself enjoying this bizarre turn of events. He was not even concerned when she tied a gag around his mouth. *"Next time,"* he thought. *"I will be in control."*

"I have one more surprise for you," Nadia said. She climbed on top of him and straddled his mid-section. Then she untied her robe and opened it for him to see. His eyes revealed puzzlement first as she was still wearing the shorts and t-shirt that she had on when she first arrived. Then his eyes revealed horror as he watched her remove a silenced pistol from a shoulder holster. He struggled to break free but the ropes and her weight upon him prevented him from escaping.

"Ahmed al-Zahar, son of Muhammad al-Zahar, brother of Ishmael al-Zahar, we know who you are and why you are here in America," Nadia calmly said to him in Arabic. "We know what you have been learning and what you intend to do with that knowledge when you return to Gaza. And we are not going to allow that to happen."

"Ahmed al-Zahar, you have committed crimes against the people of Israel," Nadia continued. "You have committed and supported acts of terror and murder against innocent people in Israel, my people.   Ten months ago, you placed a bomb in a backpack in a street café in Hadera. Your bomb killed seventeen innocent people and wounded forty-one, many of them severely. Your bomb killed and maimed innocent children.   Your victims cry out for justice against the man who murdered and maimed them." She paused, her eyes burning with rage. Then she continued, "My sister and her unborn child cry out for justice against the man who murdered them. Today, that justice will be served."

Those were the last words that Ahmed al-Zahar the engineering student / terrorist would ever hear in this life.

8 THE SOLAR-POWERED NAVY?

President Obama Announces New Solar-Powered Submarine for Navy

June 12, 2013

WASHINGTON DC: During a ceremony held in the White House Rose Garden, President Barack Obama announced plans for the development of a new solar-powered submarine for the Navy by renewable energy corporation Solyndren. "Today we embark upon a bold new course for energy efficiency and environmental friendliness for our armed forces," said the President.

Named for former Vice President Al Gore, the new class of submarines relies on solar cells mounted on the upper outer hull to charge electric batteries inside the hull which in turn propel the submarine. Re-charging the batteries will require the submarine to run on the surface for up to 12 hours a day during daylight hours.

"The Al Gore-class submarines will be able to cruise up to 100 miles on a single charge without poisoning the Earth with Greenhouse gases," said Solyndren spokesman Alan Stanford.

Currently, all U.S. submarines are nuclear-powered as are some of those in service with Britain and Russia. Many other nations' navies use diesel-electric power for their submarines. "Nuclear power entails unacceptable risks for environmental catastrophe and diesel engines cause pollutants which destroy the Ozone layer," said Under Secretary of Defense for Environmental Friendliness Chilton Templeton. "Solar power is the only logical choice for energy efficiency and environmental friendliness."

The Obama Administration plans to initially construct ten solar-powered submarines at an estimated total cost of $1 trillion. When questioned about he intends to fund the $1 trillion cost of the new submarines, President Obama replied, "We'll just borrow the money from China, like we always do. They know we're good for it."

Critics in Congress have objected to failed solar panel manufacturer Solyndren being awarded the contract without going through a formal competitive bidding process. Special White House Counsel Jessica Hawley-Smoot brushed off such criticisms by saying, "Saving the Earth must take priority over trivial laws and meaningless ethics concerns."

According to Under Secretary Templeton, the success of the solar-powered submarine will open up opportunities for other solar-powered naval ships. "We are already working on plans to convert the Navy's aircraft carriers to solar power," he said. "Their huge flight decks are acres of wasted space that would be better utilized by installing solar panels on them."

The new Al Gore-class solar-powered submarines will also have the capability of performing environmental surveillance. "The Al Gores will be able to conduct a wide range of oceanic and atmospheric testing to provide the vital scientific data we need to ensure a healthy global environment," said Under Secretary Templeton. "To provide the necessary space for the laboratory equipment, we needed to remove the submarine's weapons systems…but we believe that is a fair trade off for protecting the environment."

"The senior leaders of the Navy are absolutely furious at the colossal stupidity of trying to build a solar-powered submarine," said Commander Angela Henderson, who spoke on the condition of anonymity.

"A submarine forced to operate on the surface up to 12 hours a day to re-charge its batteries negates its primary advantage of staying hidden beneath the waves," said retired Navy Rear Admiral J. Lanford Thomas, a thirty-year veteran of the Navy's submarine force. "I would say that any idiot knows that but apparently there are some in the Obama Administration that don't."

# # #

"Navy Commissions First Solar-Powered Submarine

August 1, 2015

PORTSMOUTH, NH: Amidst the iconic musical strains of the theme for *2001: Space Odyssey*, a host of dignitaries joined with President Barack Obama and former Vice President Al Gore to witness the commissioning of the Navy's first Solar-Powered Submarine, the *USS Al Gore* (SPS-1). The traditional naval ritual was held at the Solardrone Industries' Portsmouth, New Hampshire Shipyard.

"Today we embark upon a bold new course for energy efficiency and environmental friendliness for our armed forces," said President Obama.

USS Al Gore is the very first of a new class of submarines propelled by energy derived from the Sun. Solar cells are mounted on the section of the outer hull that is above water when the submarine is running on the surface. These solar cells charge electric batteries inside the hull which in turn propels the submarine. Re-charging the batteries requires the submarine to run on the surface for up to 12 hours a day during daylight hours. According to Solardrone insiders, the solar-powered submarines will be able to cruise up to 200 miles on a single charge without poisoning the Earth with Greenhouse gases or causing a potential nuclear environmental disaster.

"For decades the Earth has been imperiled by hundreds of nuclear-powered vessels ranging all across the globe," said Under Secretary of Defense for Environmental Friendliness Dr. Chilton Templeton. "Today, the commissioning of the world's first solar-powered submarine is an important first step in our ultimate goal of ridding our planet of this monstrous menace."

Along with the revolutionary new propulsion system, the solar-powered submarines of the *Al Gore* class have an entirely new mission. Instead of maritime intelligence gathering and seeking out and destroying enemy warships, the new solar-powered submarines will perform oceanic and atmospheric surveillance.

"The *Al Gores* will conduct a wide range of oceanic and atmospheric testing to provide the vital scientific data we need to ensure a health global environment," said Under Secretary Dr. Templeton. "To provide the necessary space for the laboratory equipment, we had to remove all of the submarine's weapon systems, but I believe that is a fair trade off for protecting the environment."

Solar power manufacturer Solardrone is building the *Al Gores* at their Portsmouth, New Hampshire Shipyard – a state of the art facility constructed specifically to build the new submarines. Ten of the solar-powered submarines will initially be constructed at an estimated total cost of $2.8 trillion.

Currently, all U.S. submarines are nuclear-powered as are most of those in service with Britain and Russia. Many other nations' navies use diesel-electric power for their submarines. "Nuclear power entails unacceptable risks for environmental catastrophe and diesel engines cause pollutants which destroy the Ozone layer," said Under Secretary Dr. Templeton at the ceremony. "Solar power is the only logical choice for energy efficiency and environmental friendliness."

Critics in Congress have objected to the high cost, the unsuitability of solar power for submarines, and the award of the construction contract to failed solar panel manufacturer Solardrone without going through a formal competitive bidding process. "I asked the President how he is going to fund the $2.8 trillion cost of the new submarines," said Senator Warren Belmont of the Senate Armed Forces Committee. "He told me, 'We'll just borrow the money from China, like we always do. They know we're good for it.'"

The proposed solar-powered submarines are bewildering America's allies and emboldening America's enemies. "For many years, our nuclear submarines were very much inferior to the American submarines," said Admiral Yevgheni Prokov, commander of Russia's Northern Fleet. "President Putin asked me about these new solar-powered submarines recently. I told him, 'We don't need to worry about America's nuclear submarines anymore. They're going to get rid of them themselves!' We had a good laugh about that."

Even before *USS Al Gore*'s commissioning crew began to get her underway, Under Secretary Dr. Templeton was promoting the next project for expanding solar power throughout the Department of Defense. "Solar-powered submarines are just the first important step," said Under Secretary Dr. Templeton. "Next we will be converting the Navy's *Nimitz*-class nuclear powered aircraft carriers to solar power by covering their flight decks with solar panels."

For forty years, the nuclear-powered *Nimitz*-class super carriers have been a mainstay of American naval power. At 97,000 tons displacement and 1,092 feet in length, *Nimitz* and her sister ships are among the most massive ships in operation today. Their 4.5 acre flight decks can launch and recover up to 85 aircraft. Their nuclear reactors propel them at over 30 knots and their endurance at sea is limited only by that of their crews.

"The flight decks of our aircraft carriers are acres of wasted space," said Under Secretary Dr. Templeton. "This space is better utilized with thousands of solar cells converting the Sun's rays into clean, renewable solar electricity. Of course, covering the flight decks with solar panels will mean that the aircraft carriers will no longer be able to operate aircraft. Since modern jet aircraft produce thousands of tons of harmful air pollutants, we will also be protecting the Ozone Layer and fighting global warming by getting rid of the aircraft carrier's aircraft."

"Right now, there are countless mini-Chernobyls just waiting to happen out on the high seas," said Ban Nuclear Energy Now (BANEN) President Skye Wilde-Bayne, *USS Al Gore*'s sponsor. "Dr. Templeton's plan to convert the Navy to solar power is a huge victory for Mother Earth, us and our children!"

The assembled dignitaries and guests cheered exuberantly as *USS Al Gore* cast off her lines from the pier and was nudged out into the channel by accompanying tug boats. At 2:05 pm, she officially fired up her solar-powered propulsion system and triumphantly radioed out "Underway on solar power!" Bathed in the glow of a radiant Sun, *Al Gore* began her journey into environmentally friendly energy history. At 2:21 pm, the Sun became hopelessly obscured by clouds. Deprived of her vital energy source, *USS Al Gore* unceremoniously came to a complete stop. With no forward momentum to help her maintain buoyancy and inherently unstable due to the weight of the solar panels on her exposed deck surfaces, *USS Al Gore* rolled over and sank.

*   *   *

"Work Begins on Conversion of First Carrier to Solar-Power"

September 29, 2015

LONG BEACH, CA: The massive aircraft carrier *USS George Washington* pulled into the dry dock here at the McDougall Shipyard to begin a twenty-month conversion from nuclear-power to solar-power. "When the conversion is completed, *USS George Washington* will be the first ever aircraft carrier to be powered entirely by renewable energy and not by environmentally unfriendly nuclear energy or fossil fuels," said President Barack Obama, who was on hand for the ship's arrival.

USS George Washington is the of the *Nimitz*-class of nuclear-powered aircraft carriers. At 97,000 tons displacement and 1,092 feet in length, *USS George Washington* and her sister ships are among the most massive ships in operation today. Her acre-sized flight deck can launch and recover up to 85 aircraft.

"The flight decks of our aircraft carriers are acres of wasted space," said Under Secretary of Defense for Environmental Friendliness Chilton Templeton. "This base is better utilized with hundreds of solar cells converting the sun's rays into clean, renewable solar electricity."

Converting *USS George Washington* from nuclear to solar power is a massive undertaking that will likely cost upwards of $500 million. The conversion will require the complete removal of the nuclear reactors, the installation of fifty thousand electric batteries in their place, and the installation of ninety thousand solar cells on the flight deck.

"Of course, covering the flight deck with solar cells will mean that the aircraft carrier will not be able to operate aircraft anymore," said Under Secretary Templeton. "Since modern jet aircraft produce thousands of tons of harmful air pollutants, we will also be protecting the Ozone Layer and fighting global warming by getting rid of the aircraft carrier's aircraft."

Solar cells arrayed on nearly every available inch of the carrier's flight deck will generate electricity for the ship's propulsion system and to be stored in electric batteries for use at night and in inclement weather.
"By converting the carrier from nuclear power to solar power, we do sacrifice some speed, dropping its top speed from 30+ knots to around 10 knots…but we will be ensuring that the Amazon rain forests will be enjoyed by many generations to come," said Solyndra Vice President for Naval Technology Bart Van Der Sky.

When questioned about the high costs of converting *USS George Washington* to solar power, Under Secretary Templeton replied, "We've already wasted several trillion dollars on meaningless projects. What's another $500 million?"

USS George Washington's conversion from nuclear to solar power is a joint effort between Solyndra and McDougall Shipbuilding, neither of whom have any experience with ships as large as aircraft carriers. The contract was awarded at 3:30 am in the morning of April 3, 2015 after a ten-hour negotiating session and beer pong tournament held in the East Wing of the White House between members of the Obama Administration, and senior executives of Solyndra and McDougall Shipbuilding. Sources in the U.S. Secret Service have confirmed that the winner of the tournament was Under Secretary Templeton.

"It is exasperating that our nation's defense is being guided by idiots like Chilton Templeton," said unnamed Pentagon source Navy Commander Angela Henderson.

"The sole function of aircraft carriers is to operate combat aircraft," said retired Vice Admiral Trent Adama, former Vice Chief of Naval Operations. "An aircraft carrier without aircraft can't defend itself, let alone our nation. You have to be a brain dead Under Secretary of Defense not to know that."

# # #

9 AR RAMADI NOVEMBER 2004

"Corpsman!"

Hospitalman 2nd Class (Fleet Marine Force) Chad Devon, United States Navy, heard the call above the roar of the battle and struggled to determine it originated from. He was crouched by the side of a rundown building along a street of similar rundown buildings in a country of rundown buildings currently in the grips of a violent sectarian insurgency. Though the U.S.-led Coalition had forcibly removed Saddam Hussein and his brutal Baathist dictatorship from power a year and half earlier, much of the country remained embroiled in a violent power struggle between rival Sunni and Shia Muslims, exacerbated by hordes of foreign jihadists eager to kill in the name of Allah. Devon's company -- Alfa Company, 1st Battalion, 15th Marine Regiment – was conducting another sweep in Ar Ramadi to help wrest control of the city from Sunni insurgents.

In the streets around HM2(FMF) Devon, a small battle was raging. The sounds of weapons firing filled the air. Distinct crack sounds told Devon that some of the bullets were coming uncomfortably close to his location. Loud periodic explosions indicated that Devon's Marines were employing grenades against the insurgents; louder, less frequent explosions indicated that the insurgents were lobbing mortars haphazardly against the Marines.

"CORPSMAN UP!"

Devon struggled to his feet. He was dressed in standard issue Marine Corps Desert Marpat digital camouflage, whose seemingly random pattern of small brown and tan rectangles and squares were computer-designed to help him blend in with his surroundings. A Kevlar composite helmet protected his head and a flak vest provided some protection for his chest and torso. On his bag, he carried a forty pound pack filled with medical supplies. Strapped to his leg was a M9 Browning pistol in a drop holster. Though tradition and the Geneva Convention called for medical personnel to be unarmed, these fanatical Muslim insurgents respected neither tradition nor the Geneva Convention.

Devon was 5 feet, 9 inches tall, 180 pounds and physically fit from many months serving with Marine infantry. Nevertheless, he struggled under the weight of his gear and the effects of six hours of intense operations in this urban cesspool. With a better perception of where the call for him had originated, he began running forward in a semi-crouch towards where he thought he was needed.

"DOC, GET YOUR ASS UP HERE NOW!!"

Twenty meters ahead, he saw a Marine kneeling near the entrance to a side alley. The Marine was sweeping his rifle in the direction of the rooftops obliquely to his left. He saw the corpsman running towards him and motioned him into the alley at his back.

As HM2(FMF) Devon quickly darted past the kneeling Marine and into the alley, that Marine fired off several quick shots away from him. Up ahead, the corpsman saw a Marine kneeling next to another one laying on his back in the dirty debris-strewn alley. Just beyond them, another Marine was searching through the bullet-ridden body of an insurgent. Another Marine was twenty-five meters ahead covering the far end of the alley with a M249 Squad Automatic Weapon (SAW).

"Doc, its Ramos," said the Marine kneeling next to the fallen Marine. "The bastard jumped out of a side door. I wasn't quick enough, Doc. The mother fucker got Ramos," in a voice heavy with emotion and stress.

"It's alright, Ski, I'll take care of Ramos," Devon reassured him as he dropped down next to him. He swung his medical pack off his back and laid it beside Ramos. "Get down there and help out Jacobs with the SAW."

The Marine hesitated a few seconds then rushed down the alley to join Lance Corporal Jacobs at the far end of the alley.

Lance Corporal Ramos was having trouble breathing. His

complexion was starting to change color in a bad way. Devon ripped open the Marine's flak vest and did a quick A-B-C scan of the fallen Marine: Airway – Breathing – Circulation. A large blood spot on his left shoulder indicated a bullet wound there. Then he spotted the cause of Ramos's breathing problem: a bullet wound in his left lung. Devon immediately recognized that Ramos had a sucking chest wound – the bullet had penetrated his flak vest and punctured his left lung. Air that should have been entering and exiting through the Marine's airway passage was instead exiting out of the hole in his lung. If Devon did not act quickly, the Marine's lung would collapse.

"Hey Doc, can I help?" an unfamiliar voice asked.

HM2(FMF) Devon looked up to see a man in his thirties with a scraggy beard kneeling next to him. The man was wearing a baseball hat, blue jeans, combat boots and a knit poncho that made him look a California beach bum. Over the last four months, HM2(FMF) Devon had periodically come across members of the Navy's Sea-Air-Land (SEAL) special warfare operations teams in Ramadi. The SEALs were among America's deadliest warriors and they often dressed in rather unconventional attire. Devon surmised that the man with the scraggy beard was one of them. Though he did not appear to be carrying a weapon, that did not necessarily mean he was unarmed.

"Yeah, here, put this on his shoulder wound," Devon instructed as he handed over a compression bandage. "Keep pressure on that wound."

"Sure thing, Doc. The name's Tod," the man answered. He immediately complied with Devon's instructions.

Meanwhile, HM2(FMF) Devon wiped off the blood around Ramos's chest wound with a disinfecting pad, retrieved a special bandage designed specifically for chest wounds, removed the packaging and slapped the bandage on the bullet hole. The cellophane of the bandage adhered to the wound and sealed the hole to prevent air from escaping the wound.

Ramos's breathing improved somewhat but he still struggled. "Tod, is that bandage secured?" Devon asked.

"Yeah, Doc," the young man answered.

"Good, 'cause I gotta roll this kid," Devon answered briskly. "I think the bullet went straight through."

The young man nodded and the two of them rolled the fallen Marine onto his stomach. Tod took care to make sure that his mouth and nose remained free to breathe.

The fallen Marine was now laying on his stomach with his face pointed at the man. With one hand, he held the Marine's head; he placed two of the fingers of his other hand on the Marine's carotid artery to monitor his pulse rate.

Devon roughly pulled Ramos's flak vest completely off him. With a pair of surgical scissors, he cut open the back of his shirts. A larger wound became visible amidst dirt and blood. The corpsman quickly wiped off the area with a couple more disinfecting pads, then slapped a larger chest bandage on the hole. He made sure that the bandage was secure and gently rolled Ramos back over.

"Doc, how's Ramos doin'?"

Devon looked up to find Ramos's squad leader, Sergeant Marcos, crouched next to him. The sergeant had a grave look of concern on his face. His M16A2 rifle was resting on his knee and a pewter Crucifix was dangling off the front of his flak vest.

"We've got to get him out of here now, Sergeant," Devon answered gravely. "He's Urgent-Surgical," he added, referring to the Triage category that best described Ramos's condition. 'Urgent-Surgical' meant that Ramos needed immediate life-saving surgery.

"L-T called for a HUM-VEE to come get him," Sergeant Marcos replied. Then in Spanish he said a few words of encouragement to the fallen Marine: "Ramos, you're going to make it. Doc's patched you up and we're going to get you out of here." He then added a 'Hail Mary' prayer.

When he had finished, Sergeant Marcos noticed the young man with the beard. He stared intently into the young man's eyes for a few seconds, then sternly said, "What're you doin' here, mano?"

The young man with the beard ignored the question and simply said, "Been a long time, mano."

"Ramos's is gonna make it, Tod," Sergeant Marcos brusquely stated. "He's got two young kids. You're not taking him."

"I'm not here for him," the young man with the beard answered calmly.

The two men stared intently at each other for a few seconds. HM2(FMF) Devon was too intently focused on his patient to notice the stand-off.

Suddenly, Lance Corporal Jacobs's SAW barked to life. Sergeant Marcos looked down the alley to see Jacobs engaging an unseen target. The sergeant looked back at the young man and growled, "Doc's not going to let you take Ramos." Then he ran off down the alley to see what was happening.

"Tod, we've got to get Ramos out of here," Devon said, completely unaware of what had just transpired between the mysterious man and the Marine sergeant.

Without saying a word, the man grabbed the fallen Marine and hoisted him onto his shoulder in a fireman's carry. He stood up effortlessly despite the weight of the wounded Marine. "Lead on, Doc," he finally said.

Several more explosions occurred in rapid succession off in the distant. Gunfire burst echoed from several directions. The battle was still raging.

HM2(FMF) Devon slung his medical bag on his back and ran

down the alley with the young man carrying the wounded Marine following. A Marine at the entrance of the alley gestured to the left. Devon saw two desert-colored HUM-VEEs on the other side of the street. One of them had a subdued Red Cross painted on the side. The other sported a menacing looking turret with a fifty-caliber machine gun manned by a fiercer looking Marine. "Over there, Tod," Devon called out.

The two ran across the debris-strewn street to the medical HUM-VEE. Three Marines immediately took Ramos from the young man and placed him on a stretcher. Then with the young man's help, they placed the stretcher with Ramos on it into the back of the HUM-VEE ambulance. Another wounded Marine was on a stretcher on the opposite side of the vehicle. The doors were quickly closed and the two HUM-VEEs sped off to bring them both back to Alfa Company's base on the outskirts of Ar Ramadi. There a Navy surgical team would perform life-saving surgery on Lance Corporal Ramos and repair the damage wrought by 7.62mm bullets fired from the now dead insurgent's AK-47 assault rifle. From there, Ramos would be flown to the U.S. Army's medical center at Landstuhl, Germany for recuperation. In a few weeks, Ramos would be home with his family recovering from his near death experience.

HM2(FMF) Devon and the young man with the beard watched as the HUM-VEEs sped off. Then they started running back across the street. Suddenly, they felt the concussion and heard the boom of an explosion close by. Instinctively, Devon dropped to the ground but Tod remained standing.

Not far away, somebody yelled, "Corpsman up!"

Then somebody else yelled, "Mother fucker!"

Several other shouts resounded.

HM2(FMF) Devon spotted several Marines crouching in a circle several meters away. Over the gunfire, Devon could hear more shouting but could not make out the words. He jumped to his feet and started in their direction but the young man with the beard stopped him. "You can't help him, Doc. Not this time," he said sympathetically.

"What the fuck do you mean I can't help him?" Devon angrily shot back. "It's my fuckin' job!"

The corpsman brushed by the young man with the beard and rushed over to the circle of Marines. They were surrounding a motionless body dressed in Marine Corps MARPAT desert camouflage -- cursing and visibly upset. One Marine was kneeling beside the body, praying audibly for his soul. A large chunk of metal protruded from his chest. The lifeless face looked shockingly familiar.

Then Devon realized that he was looking at his own lifeless body. He felt a hand on his shoulder and turned to see the young man with the beard. "Tod, what the hell's goin' on?" he asked him.

"Chad, I'm Death. Your work here is done," the man with the beard replied.

10 THE LEGEND OF 'CHUG' DOLAN

Sigma Tiki Bar opened at 1 pm as usual on this balmy third Saturday in August. Located two blocks from the Atlantic Ocean in Ocean City, New Jersey, the bar consisted of a small single-story building surrounded by wooden decks, several Tiki hut outdoor bars and a large amount of sand in an effort to create an atmosphere of the South Pacific Seas at the Jersey Shore. Only copious amounts of alcohol could suspend reality sufficiently for that illusion.

For over twenty years, the Sigma Tiki Bar had hosted an annual summer gathering of alumni from Gloucester State University, a medium-sized taxpayer-supported institution of higher education located in the New Jersey suburbs of Philadelphia, Pennsylvania. Its owner and founder was a graduate of GSU who had decided to continue his raucous fraternity life-style by opening a bar at the Shore. His success was attributable to the eagerness of thousands of other college graduates and college students to overindulge in his wide selection of alcohol products while vacationing at the Shore.

As was their custom, Kevin Mikulski, Justin "JB" Brown, Vincent "Vinny" DeLeo and Edward Larson arrived promptly at the bar's opening. The official festivities did not kick off until 4 p.m. but the four GSU / Beta Tau fraternity alumni always arrived early to spend the afternoon reminiscing about their college glory days before the main crowd showed up.

The four friends were the survivors of a group of six young men who matriculated at GSU as freshmen ten years previously. The six had been suite mates in the dorm for their first year of college. That fall semester, they had all pledged Beta Tau fraternity, one of the most notorious Greek organizations at GSU. They lived together in the Beta Tau House for two years. After that, somehow they managed to graduate and enter the work force. These four remained in contact, getting together several times a year in a vain attempt to relive their ill-spent collegiate days.

The owner was well acquainted with the four men. He warmly greeted them upon their arrival and escorted them to an outdoor table overlooking a sand volleyball court. Turning to a passing waitress, he said, "Make sure these guys don't run dry. Their first two pitchers are on the house." Then to his guests, he said, "If you need anything else, just say it."

"Actually, we need a bottle of Jack," Kevin Mikulski reminded him.

"Right, I almost forgot," the owner apologized. "Sandy, get me a bottle of Jack."

Sandy soon returned with a bottle of Jack Daniels Scotch Whiskey and a tray of empty shot glasses.

"Allow me gentlemen," the owner said, as he took the bottle and opened it for them. Then he filled five of the shot glasses and passed them around, keeping one for himself.

"To Stumpy," Kevin said raising his shot glass.

"To Stumpy," the other men replied, quickly downing the liquor. The owner poured another round which was consumed just as quickly as the first.

Bruce 'Stumpy' Mitchell was one of the two missing members of the original six friends. His nickname was an obvious reference to his short, squat stature. 'Stumpy' had remained a part of the periodic gatherings for three years after graduation until being killed in a drunk driving accident --- a painful reminder that alcohol, motor vehicles and large trees were not good combinations. The only fortunate aspect of Stumpy's untimely death was that he had not taken anyone else with him into Eternity. Every year, in a seemingly defiant salute to Stumpy's alcohol-caused demise, the four friends drank the first round of shots in his memory.

The owner excused himself to attend to other business and the four friends got down to the serious business of renewing their friendship with the active support of various alcoholic beverages.

"So who do we know is coming today?" Vinny DeLeo asked.

"I've been checking on Facebook," Kevin Mikulski answered. He had long-since assumed responsibility for prodding Beta Tau alumni and their universe of friends to attend this annual debacle. "And so far, it looks like, Keith Sommers, Andy Stevens, Andy O'Connor, Karen, Jessica, Tammy, Wolfman, Big Pete, Black Haired Kelly, Red Haired Kelly and Taylor from Theta Rho, the whole Phi class, Bill Davis ---"

"The whole Phi class?" Edward Larson interrupted. "You mean Max and Zito?" Beta Tau's pledge classes always had at least six pledges with the noticeable exception of the Phi class which had only two pledges.

"Yeah, Max and Zito - the whole Phi class – are both coming," Kevin retorted with unconcealed annoyance. "As I was saying, we have Bill Davis, the Omega class minus Bill Micelli, five of the six Alpha Betas, and Donna Elliott and a bunch of her Zeta sisters. Did I miss anyone?"

"Is Donna bringing her kids again this year?" Ed asked to start things off.

"You mean Delta Donna, the chick who hooked up with damn near every guy in Delta Tau?" Justin Brown replied, already knowing the answer.

"She only brought her twins once....a few years ago when she couldn't find a babysitter," Vince interjected in her defense. "It worked out well. The twins slept most of the night and she had a carrier for her wine coolers!"

"Marty Stein's coming," "JB" Brown informed his group. "His divorce is finalized and he told me he wants to make up for the years he lost while he was married."

"I talked to Sid Bascom last week," said Vinny. His voice turned to condescension. "His wife's still mad at him for last year's reunion so she booked a Disney cruise for her, the kids and him for this week." He finished off his first beer. "They should be pulling into Grand Bahama right about now."

That brought some catcalls and sneers from the other three men. "My wife would never do that," Ed commented arrogantly. "She won't come to these events anymore but she knows better than to try and stop me from coming."

"Where's Jackie, JB?" Vinny asked.

JB finished off his first beer and poured another. "She went to her sister's house in the Poconos," he answered. "Good place for her. She's been real moody lately. I'm probably going to dump her after Labor Day."

Having accounted for most everyone in their group of college-era friends, the four men turned their attention to their past exploits while students at GSU. The next hour was spent reliving and retelling stories that had been relived and retold dozens of times since the events that inspired them had actually occurred. In the blur of alcohol and the fading of memories, the facts of these stories often became equally blurred and faded. Anthropologists would say that this was how legends and myths are created.

Inevitably, the conversation turned to the other missing member of the original six freshmen. Ed asked the obligatory question, "Anyone heard from Chug?" No one answered.

Sean Francis Dolan was more commonly known as "Chug" for his extraordinary ability to consume large quantities of alcohol given his small, five-foot, six-inch stature and slim build. Chug had never attended one of these gatherings. In fact, no one had seen or heard from him since graduation. Every year, it seemed less and less likely that he would ever attend.

Then in what had become an annual tradition, speculation began on his whereabouts. Various theories, each one intentionally more bizarre than its predecessors, were put forth. "He's working on Wall Street for Goldman Sachs," JB theorized.

"Nobody in their right mind would ever trust Chug with their money," Ed countered.

"I thought I saw him at Philly International a few weeks ago screening passengers for TSA," Vinny D corrected JB.

"No, you're both wrong," Kevin countered. "He's working as a mountain guide in Tibet. I caught a glimpse of him on *Conquering Everest* on the Discovery Channel two weeks ago."

"Pound for pound, nobody could out drink Chug," Vinny said. "I remember when he first showed up at GSU. He was quiet, almost mousy, didn't say much. But a week later, he was a completely different person. I rarely got home from a party after him."

"Yeah," JB chimed in. "His transformation was astounding. One week, he's barely noticeable in an empty room, the next week he's doing keg stands and raising hell. The kid really came into his own at college."

"Alright, new game. This time, real money's involved," Kevin said with a tone that was more of an order than a suggestion. "Twenty bucks a head. Whoever has the best Chug story takes the pot. Open your wallets, gentlemen."

"Wait, Kevin, who's going to judge this? We need someone impartial," Ed objected.

"Twenty bucks? That's insulting. Make it fifty!" JB admonished.

"Hey guys. How's everybody doing?" Karen Emrich announced as she walked up to the table.

"Fifty's more like it," Vinny added.

"Hey, Karen -- I'm good with fifty," Ed concurred.

"What are you guys doing?" Karen asked, trying to make sense of the rapid fire discussion into which she had just stumbled.

"We're running a pool on who has the best Chug story," Vinny informed her, as he pulled out a fifty dollar bill from his wallet and threw it on the table. "I'm in. There's my President Grant."

"Here's mine," Ed said, throwing another fifty dollar bill on the table. "Hey, Karen, we need a judge. You're it!"

Before Karen could object, Vinny was pulling over a chair and roughly guiding her into it.

"Glad to see you Karen," said Kevin, thrusting a beer in front of her. "You look thirsty. Have a beer."

Now seated, Karen looked around the table. She grabbed bills, quickly counted them and then stacked them in front of her. She took a long drink from the cup of beer that had been placed before her. "Who's first?" she asked after putting the cup down.

"I'll go," Kevin answers. He downed a shot of Jack and began his best Chug story. "Chug was dating this girl Angela, Spring semester, Junior Year. They get in a huge fight. She won't talk to him. She won't answer her phone or answer her door. This goes on for a few days. So finally one night after trying yet again to get her to answer her door, he goes outside and scales the side of her apartment building."

"Angela lived on the third floor of that building," Vinny interrupted. "How the hell did he do that?"

"You remember, her building had balconies," Kevin explained.

"So he pulled himself up to the second floor balcony below her apartment, balanced on that one's railing, then pulled himself up to her balcony. For his size, Chug was strong so the hard part wasn't the climbing. It was balancing on the railing to reach her balcony. Anyway, he climbs onto her balcony and opens the sliding door, scaring the hell out of her. But she calms down when he gives a dozen roses and they make up."

"How did he climb while a dozen roses in his hands?" Karen asked.

"He held them in his teeth as he climbed," Kevin answered.

"There's no way that happened! You stole that story from a Spider Man comic book!" Vinny countered.

"It sure did happen. I know. I was there," Kevin retorted. He took a long drink from his beer. "I was in bed with Angela's roommate at the time."

"Cheryl Amato? You did Cheryl?" Ed asked.

"It might have been her," Kevin answered. "I can't remember her name. We only hooked up a couple times."

In the meantime, two more women joined the discussion: Jessica Ellison and Tammy Clark-Raynes. "Hey guys, how's it going?" Jessica greeted them.

Instantly Vinny brought over two more chairs to the table and shots were placed before the new arrivals. "We're telling Chug stories," Kevin explained. "These'll start you off."

The two new additions to the discussion slammed the proffered liquor and joined in the reminiscing.

Vince "Vinny" DeLeo was next to offer his best recollection about 'Chug' Dolan. "Me and Chug are working the door one night Junior year," he began. "Victor Mason, from Kappa Rho, you remember, the guy who curled his own hair. Well, Vic is scamming on some freshman girl. He's laying it on heavy about what a great wrestler he is --- two-time State Champion in high school for his weight class, wrestling scholarship to GSU, tried out for the Olympic Team, and so on. Chug and I listen to this garbage for a few minutes. Then without saying a word he puts down his beer, walks over to Vic and does a leg sweep on him. Now Vic had about thirty pounds on Chug but Chug sends him down hard. Vic balls up like a turtle and now Chug is standing over top of him and he says, and I quote, 'You're not such a good wrestler.'"

The table erupted in laughter and howls. "A leg sweep??! Where did Chug learn how to do a leg sweep?" asked Kevin as he downed another shot of Jack.

"Sophomore year, he took judo or ji-jitsu or something like that. I don't remember exactly what but I'll never forget the look of sheer terror on Vic's face!" Vinny answered.

"Your turn Ed," Karen announced. "Make it a good one."

"Chug and I are going back to the dorm after a pledge function and we're both hammered, I mean hammered," Ed starts off. He finishes his beer and pours another one for himself. "So we're coming by the lake behind Abbott Hall and for some reason, Chug decides to jump in the lake. The next morning, he wakes me up at 8 am and says, 'Dude, why am I all covered in mud?' And I answer, 'Because you went in the lake last night.' He says 'Oh'. Next thing I know, he's showered, dressed and heading out the door. I'm like, 'Dude, what are you doing?' He says, 'Going to class. I got a chemistry exam.' He ended up getting like a 95 or something on the exam."

"Chug got a three point seven GPA while we were pledging," Kevin remembered. "That was his lowest GPA ever."

"He got a three-seven while pledging?!?" Jessica asked in disbelief. "The best I did was a three-one. I got a two-five when I pledged."

"Chug was unbelievable," Ed added. "He would drink until 2 am, get up for a 9 am class and not be hung over. He missed one class in the two years that I lived with him."

"'Study hard, drink hard' is what he used to say," Tammy remembered.

Karen added, "I would have failed biology if it weren't for him…and he wasn't even a bio major!"

"I took a bunch of classes that he was taking because I knew he would help me get at least a B plus and he always he did," Tammy said.

"Alright, back to business, gentlemen," JB stated emphatically. "Just give me the money now because this story beats all."

The other three men responded with howls of disapproval. Karen hushed them. "Okay, JB, you better be able to back up that claim."

"Late October of Senior Year, Chug and I go into the city one Monday night," JB begins. "We're at this bar on South Street, an Irish place called Ring of Kerry. We're sitting up at the bar when this blonde comes up next to Chug and starts asking him about his soccer jersey. Chug answers that it's a German World Cup Soccer Team jersey. She asks, 'Where'd you get it?" and Chug answers, 'Germany.' So then she asks, 'Oh, are you from Germany?'" And you know Chug, when he sees an opportunity to mess with someone, he grabs onto it. So Chug starts talking like Mike Myers in the old Saturday Night Live Sprockets skit, and answers that his name is Dieter and he's an exchange student from Dusseldorf."

"Dieter from Dusseldorf?" Tammy asks incredulously. "Is that even a real place?"

"Yeah, Chug did a summer study abroad in Germany the summer after Junior Year," JB answers. "It turns out the blonde is with a group of her friends from some sorority at UPENN celebrating another girl's birthday. She invites us to join them at their table, which of course, we do. We go over to the table. There's five of them there. One of the girls, her name was Dana, or Diane,

Debbie, no, Dana, that's it.   Anyway Dana is an international business major and she's having trouble with her Intermediate German class and so she starts asking Chug, aka 'Dieter,' all kinds of questions about the German language.   Chug is answering her questions in both English and in perfect German -- still with the Mike Myers Sprockets voice. The conversation turns from Dana's language class to Dieter's life story.   And here's where I nearly lost it. Dieter, Chug, tells these girls that he was originally born in East Germany, that his father was a fighter pilot in the East German air force and that when he was five years old, his father stole a MIG fighter jet and flew his family to West Germany to escape Communism. They had to change their names because the East German secret police tried to kill his father in retaliation for stealing the MIG and defecting to the West.   We spend over an hour, drinking and hanging out with these girls. I can't believe these girls are falling for this. Anyway, next thing I know, Chug's going home with Dana."

The group of friends is by now laughing uncontrollably at JB's story. "I think JB wins the pot," Jessica finally catches her breath.

"No, wait, it gets better," JB admonishes her.   "Three days later…." He pauses for effect. "Three days later, Chug comes back to our apartment wearing a UPENN sweatshirt and carrying a UPENN duffle bag. I'm like 'Dude, where've you been?' He says, 'Helping Dana study for her mid-terms.' Then he proceeds to fill me in on what's happened the last three days. Turns out, Chug goes back to Dana's apartment. They get romantic. He sleeps over. The next day, she wants to him to stay longer. She takes him shopping, and buys him some clean clothes, and some hygiene items. Then she takes him to class with her. She introduces him around campus as 'Dieter from Dusseldorf.' She takes him *to her Intermediate German class*! The class that day was being taught by a Graduate Assistant, who takes an immediate liking to 'Dieter' and asks him to share his experiences as a German university student with the class. Chug hangs out with Dana, and helps her study for her mid-terms, among other things. By the third day, 'Dieter' has gained some notoriety on campus."

The laughter at the table is deafening. "How did he pull that one off?" Vinny asks when he is able to speak.

"Like I said, Chug had studied in Germany for a couple months and he had taken four semesters of German before that," JB answered. "And Chug was always quick on his feet. But this charade started getting bigger than even he could handle. So he got out of there before it blew up in his face. He comes back to GSU. Dana ended up ace-ing her German mid-term thanks to 'Dieter.'"

"That's too funny!" Kevin interjected. "You win. Karen, give'em the cash."

"Did Dieter, I mean Chug, ever see Dana again?" Tammy asked.

"No, she asked him to come back to PENN and help her study for her German final, but Chug told her he couldn't because his student visa was expiring soon," JB explained.

"And nobody found out the truth?" Karen asked.

"No one," answered JB.

"Karen, you've heard the stories," Ed said. "I think it's obvious who wins the pot."

"It was a tough decision but I have to go with Chug's UPENN adventure," Karen answered. "Only Chug could pull something like that off."

JB jumped from his chair in triumph and grabbed up the pile of cash on the table. Vinny, Kevin and Ed all conceded defeat and the conversation resumed.

"Has anyone seen or heard from Chug lately?" asked Jessica.

"Lately?!? Lately?" Kevin replied condescendingly. "JB's the only one who's seen or heard him since the night before graduation!" He finished off his latest beer. "JB, tell the girls *that* story."

"Well, as you'll recall, we all went over to Tammy's after the Senior Week trip to South Street," JB explained. "At some point, he left."

"That's right, I tried to get him to sleep over but he insisted on going back to his place," Tammy added.

"I crashed on Tammy's couch, woke up and went to graduation still hung over," JB continued. "After I got my diploma, I ran into him. He was all cleaned up, looking like a GQ ad. I said, 'Chug, where you been? What happened last night?' And as calm as can be, he says, 'I saw Jesus this morning.' That was it. No explanation, nothing. He walked off and I haven't seen him or heard from him since. Nobody has."

"That's so bizarre," Jessica said in reply. "Do you think he'd show up today?"

"Not a chance," JB answered. "I can't explain it but there was something very strange about him."

"Was he tripping?" Jessica asked.

"No way," JB answered. "I knew him all four years at GSU and lived with him for three of those years. He never touched the stuff or any other drug for that matter."

"Yeah, whenever anyone would offer stuff to him, he'd always reply with something like 'No, I'm doing enough damage to my body with alcohol," Vinny added.

"Good evening, ladies and gentlemen. Got room any here?"

Draws dropped as the four friends and their compatriots saw Sean "Chug" Dolan standing before them. He was dressed in a khaki pants with a maroon Loyola University New Orleans polo shirt. His graying brown hair was cropped short. Then a chorus of voices greeted him, the words all jumbling together in an incoherent cacophony.

"Hey, relax, everybody, its just me, not the Pope," Chug said. The friends all jumped to their feet. Hugs and handshakes were exchanged. Everyone was talking at once, absolutely mystified by Chug's unexpected appearance.

After a few minutes, a chair was brought over for the latest addition to the troupe of revelers. "We all want to know," said Kevin. "Chug, where've you been since graduation?" Everyone at the table voiced their agreement.

"Short answer, Philly, now New Orleans," Chug answered cryptically.

"You live in New Orleans!? Dude, we're coming down for Mardi Gras!" JB interrupted. Several shouts of approval erupted.

"What's the long answer, Chug?" Tammy asked. "What happened after you left my apartment before graduation?"

"Hey Chug, your hands are empty. You don't have a beer," Kevin asked.

"Yes, I know," Chug replied nonchalantly. "As you'll recall...which I do somewhat...we went to South Street and closed the place down. We had all chipped in on a van service to get us there and back so no one had to drive. I think we got back to Tammy's around three-thirty or four."

"That sounds right," Karen agreed. "I don't remember anything after that until the next morning."

"Well, the last thing I remember was leaving Tammy's to go back to my apartment," Chug continued. "Then I'm waking up in the front pew of Saint Jude's Church and Jesus is staring me in the face. I don't know how I got in there. I had walked by that church a thousand times and never had been inside until that morning."

"You broke into a church and passed out in a pew?!" Ed roared. "That beats all!" Others erupted in laughter and howls too. Some congratulatory comments were uttered.

"I don't know how I got in the church but the doors must have been open because nothing was broken," Chug clarified.

"You told me after graduation that you saw Jesus, and I didn't know what you were talking about," JB interjected. "I still don't."

"I did see Jesus that morning," Chug replied. "I woke up in front of a statue of Jesus with the image of the Sacred Heart on his chest. And Jesus spoke to me. He said, 'You're wasting your life, Sean. Follow me and I'll save you.'"

"The statue spoke to you?" Vinny asked. "Man, you must still have been drunk."

"Not the statue -- Jesus," Chug calmly answered. "Jesus spoke into my heart and said, 'You're wasting your life, Sean. Follow me and I'll save you.'"

"Save you from what, Chug, the priest when he shows up and finds you drunk in his church?" Ed interrupted. Kevin, Jessica and Vince all burst out laughing.

"From hell," Chug answered with an intense look on his face. "Jesus wanted to save me from eternal damnation."

"So what did you do?" Karen asked.

"I decided to follow Jesus," Chug answered. He returned to telling his story. "Well, then a priest shows up. I look at my watch and its seven-thirty a.m. Apparently daily Mass is at eight. Jesus's words are still ringing in my head. I had not been to Mass or Confession since high school, not even for Christmas. I walk over to the priest, Father Benedict, and I tell him everything that has happened up to that point: the partying, the drinking, how I woke up in his church and what Jesus had just said to me and I tell him I want to follow Jesus. He offers me absolution. I stay for Mass then head back to the apartment, shower, get into decent clothes, and pack my stuff in my truck. All my drinking paraphernalia and souvenirs of my sinful existence go into a dumpster. I go to graduation and then leave GSU for good. That fall I entered St. Charles Borromeo Seminary in Philly. I got ordained as a priest five years later, moved to New Orleans and now I'm teaching Theology at Loyola University."

Father Sean finished his story and for a few moments no one spoke at the table. Finally, JB reached into his pocket and pulled out a wad of fifties. He handed it over to him, saying, "We had a contest before on who had the best story about you. You win with that one. Whether its true or not, that's the best drunk story I've ever heard!"

The table erupted in laughter. "Somebody get Chug a beer!" Kevin commanded.

Ed filled a cup with beer and set it before Chug. Chug ignored it.

"JB just told us the UPENN story, which was hysterical but this one, you being a priest and all, this one tops that by far!" Vinny commended him.

"You really had us going there," Kevin added. "We didn't know what to believe. You drop off the planet for ten years and show up here claiming to be a priest. That's a story of epic proportions! You're not buying a single drink tonight, Chug. It's all on me!"

"You ought to be working in Hollywood," Jessica said admiringly. "You could win an Oscar with that performance!"

The group of friends erupted in laughter and side conversations.

"Guys, Chug's story is true," Tammy spoke up, trying to be heard over the laughter. "I just Googled his name. Look..."

Tammy held up her iPhone. On the display was a photo and brief biography of Father Sean Francis Dolan posted on the Loyola University website.

Various exhortations of disbelief were voiced by those gathered at the table as one by one they viewed the images on Tammy's iPhone.

"Hey, that was just posted yesterday," Ed observed. "I've Googled your name before and never found anything."

"I've been keeping a low profile," Father Sean explained.

When reality finally penetrated through the haze of the afternoon's alcohol consumption, the friends were thunderstruck to realize that their binge-drinking, hard partying frat boy friend had in fact become a priest in the Catholic Church. They sat speechless at the revelation of this unbelievable turn of events.

Finally, Kevin spoke up with unconcealed disapproval in his voice, "So, Chug, I mean, Father Sean, what are you doing here in a bar?"

"I'm here to save sinners for Jesus," the frat boy turned priest replied. "I'm here to help Jesus save you all…from hell."

ABOUT THE AUTHOR

Bryan J. Dickerson is a military historian specializing in World War II. He holds a Bachelor's of Arts degree in History from Rowan University and a Master's of Arts degree in American History from Monmouth University. A former U.S. Navy Reserve Religious Program Specialist 1st Class (Fleet Marine Force), he mobilized and deployed twice to Iraq for Operation Iraqi Freedom. He is also former Squadron Historian for Marine Wing Support Squadron (MWSS) 472. He is the author of *The Liberators of Pilsen: The U.S. Army 16th Armored Division in World War Two Czechoslovakia* published by McFarland and Company of Jefferson, NC, and five other books published through Kindle Direct Publishing: *Marine General from the Ranks: The Life of Lt Gen Homer L. Litzenberg Jr., Modern Saints and Blesseds of the Catholic Church, The Organized Marine Corps Reserve in World War Two, An Anthology of Military and Cold War History,* and the *History of Marine Wing Support Squadron 472.* He, his wife Lisa and their children live in Gloucester County, NJ.